Memories of Childhood

This is number

84 of 5000

of a limited edition signed by the artist

Michael Foreman

MICHAEL FOREMAN

Memories of Childhood

The Classic Stories
War Boy and *After the War Was Over*

PAVILION

DEDICATION

To my brothers and our Mum

Memories of Childhood comprises *War Boy*
originally published in 1989 by PAVILION BOOKS LIMITED
and *After the War Was Over*
originally published in 1995 by PAVILION BOOKS LIMITED

This combined edition first published in 2000 in Great Britain by
PAVILION BOOKS LIMITED
London House, Great Eastern Wharf
Parkgate Road, London SW11 4NQ
www.pavilionbooks.co.uk

Designed by Janet James

A CIP catalogue record for this book is available
from the British Library.

ISBN 1 86205 408 8

Set in Gill Sans
Printed in Italy by Giunti Industrie Grafiche

2 4 6 8 10 9 7 5 3 1

This book can be ordered direct from the publisher. Please contact
the Marketing Department. But try your bookshop first.

Contents

■ ■ ■ ■

WAR BOY

A Country Childhood

TO MY BROTHERS AND OUR MUM

This edition published in Great Britain in 1991 by
PAVILION BOOKS LIMITED
London House, Great Eastern Wharf, Parkgate Road,
London SW11 4NQ

First published in hardback in 1989

Copyright © Michael Foreman 1989

Designed by Janet James

A CIP catalogue record for this book is available from
The British Library

ISBN 1 85145 704 6

10 9 8 7 6 5 4

Printed and bound in Italy by
Giunti Industrie Grafiche, Prato

I woke up when the bomb came through the roof.
It came through at an angle, overflew my bed by
inches, bounced up over my mother's bed, hit the
mirror, dropped into the grate and exploded up the
chimney. It was an incendiary. A fire-bomb.

My brother Ivan appeared in pyjamas and his Home Guard
tin hat. Being in the Home Guard, he had ensured that all
the rooms in our house were stuffed with sandbags. Ivan
threw sand over the bomb but the dry sand kept sliding
off. He threw the hearthrug over the bomb and jumped
up and down on it, until brother Pud arrived with a
bucket of wet sand from the yard. This did the trick.

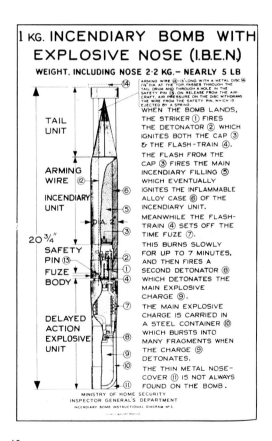

1 KG. **INCENDIARY BOMB WITH EXPLOSIVE NOSE (I.B.E.N.)**

WEIGHT, INCLUDING NOSE 2·2 KG. – NEARLY 5 LB

TAIL UNIT

ARMING WIRE ⑫

INCENDIARY UNIT

20¾"

SAFETY PIN ⑬

FUZE BODY

DELAYED ACTION EXPLOSIVE UNIT

ARMING WIRE ⑫ 13" LONG WITH A METAL DISC ⑭ 1¼" DIA AT THE TOP, PASSES THROUGH THE TAIL DRUM AND THROUGH A HOLE IN THE SAFETY PIN ⑬. ON RELEASE FROM THE AIR-CRAFT, AIR PRESSURE ON THE DISC WITHDRAWS THE WIRE FROM THE SAFETY PIN, WHICH IS EJECTED BY A SPRING.

WHEN THE BOMB LANDS, THE STRIKER ① FIRES THE DETONATOR ② WHICH IGNITES BOTH THE CAP ③ & THE FLASH-TRAIN ④.

THE FLASH FROM THE CAP ③ FIRES THE MAIN INCENDIARY FILLING ⑤ WHICH EVENTUALLY IGNITES THE INFLAMMABLE ALLOY CASE ⑥ OF THE INCENDIARY UNIT.

MEANWHILE THE FLASH-TRAIN ④ SETS OFF THE TIME FUZE ⑦.

THIS BURNS SLOWLY FOR UP TO 7 MINUTES, AND THEN FIRES A SECOND DETONATOR ⑧ WHICH DETONATES THE MAIN EXPLOSIVE CHARGE ⑨.

THE MAIN EXPLOSIVE CHARGE IS CARRIED IN A STEEL CONTAINER ⑩ WHICH BURSTS INTO MANY FRAGMENTS WHEN THE CHARGE ⑨ DETONATES.

THE THIN METAL NOSE-COVER ⑪ IS NOT ALWAYS FOUND ON THE BOMB.

MINISTRY OF HOME SECURITY
INSPECTOR GENERAL'S DEPARTMENT
INCENDIARY BOMB INSTRUCTIONAL DIAGRAM Nº3

CHURCHMAN'S CIGARETTES

TWO-MEN PORTABLE MANUAL FIRE-PUMP IN ACTION

CHURCHMAN'S CIGARETTES

A CHAIN OF BUCKETS

CHURCHMAN'S CIGARETTES

REMOVAL OF INCENDIARY BOMB WITH SCOOP AND HOE

CHURCHMAN'S CIGARETTES

INCENDIARY BOMB COOLING DOWN

CHURCHMAN'S CIGARETTES

EXTINCTION OF INCENDIARY BOMB

CHURCHMAN'S CIGARETTES

CONTROL OF INCENDIARY BOMB

If you had collected enough cigarette cards you knew what to do.

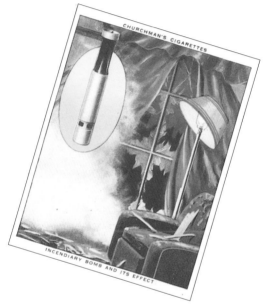

CHURCHMAN'S CIGARETTES

INCENDIARY BOMB AND ITS EFFECT

Mother grabbed me from the bed. The night sky was
filled with lights. Searchlights, anti-aircraft fire, stars and a
bombers' moon. The sky bounced as my mother ran. Just
as we reached our dug-out across the street, the sky
flared red as the church exploded.

It was Monday, April 21 1941, just before 10 p.m. Thousands of incendiaries were dropped on our village, Pakefield, and the neighbouring big town, Lowestoft. The Germans were trying to set alight the thatched roof of the church to make a beacon for the following waves of bombers. Within a few minutes more than forty fires were blazing in Pakefield and the southern part of Lowestoft. Two incendiaries buried themselves in the roof of the church. The Rector climbed ladders to extinguish one, but was unable to reach the other.

The high explosive bombs followed immediately. More were dropped in this raid than in any other, but with the church now blazing, a thick mist rolled up from the sea and ruined the bombers' night. The following waves of bombers turned back.

14

We were safe. And we were together. We were three brothers and Mum. Ivan, Bernard (known to us only as Pud) and myself. (Our father had died one month before I was born.) Also with us was Aunt Louie.

In the morning we returned home. Mum went to the loo, which was outside in the yard, and found a hole in the roof and a bomb, unexploded, in the floor. Pud pulled it out and carried it to 'Pal' the policeman in the police box on the corner.

'Young Bernard!!'

My big brother Ivan worked in a garage. Brother Pud went to school every day in a nearby village, as the local school was full of soldiers.

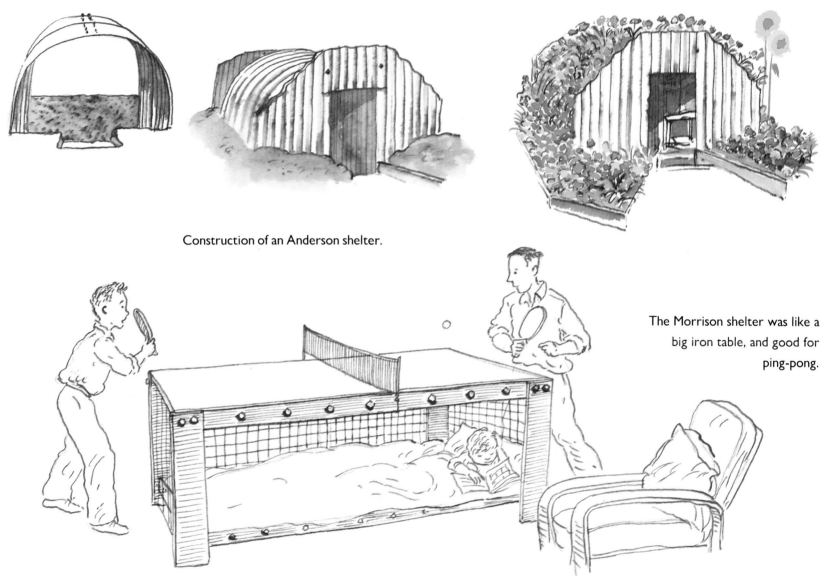

Construction of an Anderson shelter.

The Morrison shelter was like a big iron table, and good for ping-pong.

17

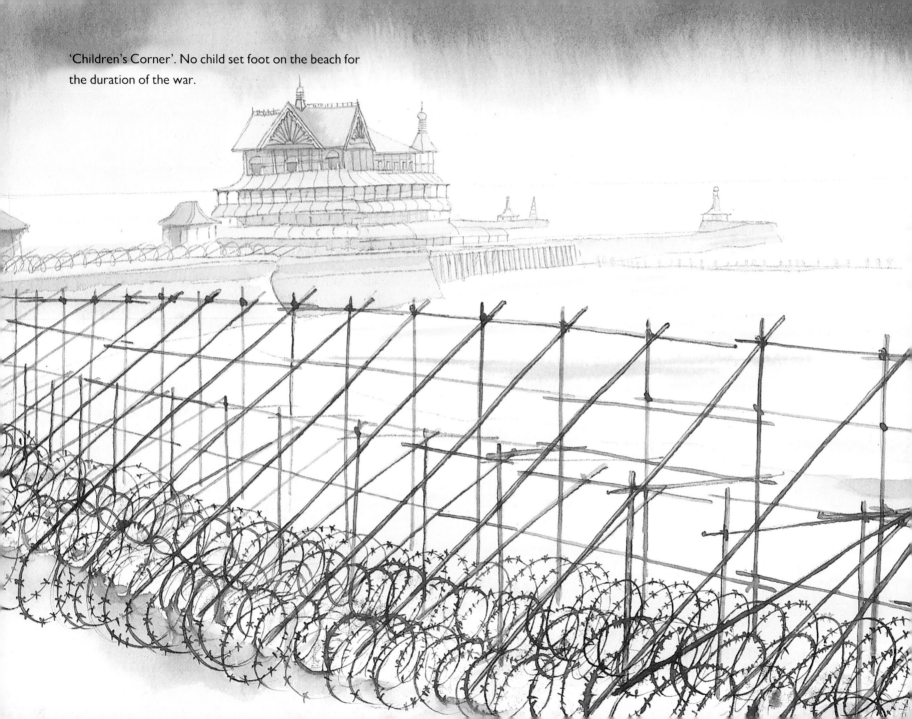

'Children's Corner'. No child set foot on the beach for
the duration of the war.

THE FRONT LINE

Lowestoft was a front line target throughout the war because it was a very large naval base and headquarters to the Minesweeping Service. It was Britain's nearest town to Germany, and after the fall of Holland the Germans had airfields only ninety miles away. Lowestoft and the surrounding area became a practice ground for the Luftwaffe, just a twenty-minute hop to the virtually defenceless coast.

Britain's defences were concentrated around Dover and the Channel ports. When France fell in 1940, Lowestoft did not have a single gun. Fake guns were installed. The first real guns to arrive were two 1917 field guns with wooden wheels. The very young gun crews lived in holiday beach huts.

The sea defences, scaffold poles and barbed wire, stretched as far as the eye could see along the beach. Mines were hidden in the sand. Concrete blockhouses or pillboxes squatted along the cliff-top.

At Pakefield we had a massive gun emplacement with a fake gun – three scaffold poles strapped together and covered with camouflage netting. (The netting mysteriously disappeared one night and suddenly Bumshie Fuller had a strangely coloured shrimp trawl net.)

Further along the cliff at the old Pakefield holiday camp were more gun emplacements which eventually had real guns, but initially were just piles of fish-boxes filled with sand. More real guns were on the cliff next to the Palais de Dance and the Grand Hotel (which served as the Czech Army Headquarters).

Lowestoft was ringed with anti-tank blocks and deep ditches called tank traps which rapidly filled with water. (Brother Pud and friends caught sticklebacks and newts in Easy's pond and stocked up all the tank traps. Thereafter the local boys had a multitude of fishing places in addition to the two or three traditional ponds.)

Pillboxes lurked in hedgerows and at cross-roads. Some pillboxes were disguised as haystacks and stood about innocently beside country roads. Others along the coast pretended to be holiday chalets or ice-cream stalls.

At the beginning of the Black Out there were more casualties from road accidents than from enemy actions. White lines were painted along kerbs and men were encouraged to leave their white shirt tails hanging out at night. A local farmer painted white stripes on his cows in case they strayed onto the roads.

Lowestoft's population was reduced by two-thirds when most of the children and many of the mums were evacuated. Some went to stay with relatives in safer inland towns and villages, but many children were sent to distant places and spent the years of the war with people they had never seen before.

On June 2 1940, 2,969 children left in five special trains. 'Danger of Invasion' posters were pasted up everywhere, and all people not needed for the running of the town were advised to leave for a safer place. Many refused to go, including, of course, our mum. But she did send brother Pud to stay with our Granny who ran a pub in rural Norfolk. He stuck it for a month or two, then sniffed out a fish lorry and got a lift back to Lowestoft fish market and a bus home.

'What on earth are you doing home?' said our Mum.

'I want to go fishing,' replied Pud.

'Well, that's that,' said Mum, 'if we are going to be blown up, we'll be blown up together.'

IMPORTANT NOTICE

EVACUATION

The public throughout the country generally are being told to "stay put" in the event of invasion. For military reasons, however, it will in the event of attack be necessary to remove from this town all except those persons who have been specially instructed to stay. An order for the compulsory evacuation of this town will be given when in the judgment of the Government it is necessary, and plans have been arranged to give effect to such an order when it is made.

You will wish to know how you can help NOW in these plans.

THOSE WHO ARE ENGAGED IN WORK OF ANY DESCRIPTION IN THE TOWN SHOULD STAY FOR THE PRESENT.

OTHER PERSONS SHOULD, SO FAR AS THEY ARE ABLE TO DO SO, MAKE ARRANGEMENTS TO LEAVE THE TOWN—PARTICULARLY

    MOTHERS WITH YOUNG CHILDREN
    SCHOOL CHILDREN
    AGED AND INFIRM PERSONS
    PERSONS WITHOUT OCCUPATION OR IN RETIREMENT.

All such persons who can arrange for their accommodation with relatives or friends in some other part of the country should do so. Assistance for railway fares and accommodation will be given to those who require it.

Advice and, where possible, assistance will be given to persons who desire to leave the town but are unable to make their own arrangements.

Information about these matters can be obtained from the local Council Offices.

(*Signed*) **WILL SPENS,**
Regional Commissioner for Civil Defence.

CAMBRIDGE,
   2nd July, 1940.

(393/4177) Wt. 19544-30 125M 7/40 H & S Ltd. **Gp. 393**

CHURCHMAN'S CIGARETTES

THE CIVILIAN RESPIRATOR—HOW TO ADJUST IT

THE CIVILIAN RESPIRATOR—HOW TO REMOVE IT

People gave up carrying masks after a few months. We were taught to spit on the inside of the mica window to prevent it misting up. Gas masks were good for rude noises and fogged up anyway.

Hitler will send no warning –

so always carry your gas mask

ISSUED BY THE MINISTRY OF HOME SECURITY

THE SHOP

Our mother ran the village shop. She sold everything, from sweets to sealing wax and string. The pavement outside was piled high with vegetables. Inside, the shop always seemed full of legs. Khaki legs, sailors' legs, busmen's legs and, worst of all, little old ladies' legs. I had a horror of being trapped under voluminous dark skirts smelling of rotten lavender and cats' pee.

Our home and shop stood with two other little houses on a kind of triangular traffic island surrounded by three roads. It was at the end of the bus route from town, and after turning the buses around, the drivers and conductors had five minutes' break.

Mother made tea in a great big pot, and the busmen drank it from saucers as they couldn't wait for it to cool.

The soldiers and sailors had more time. They stood about the shop and joked and told stories while they drank their tea, saucer in one hand, cup in the other and a ciggy smouldering between two fingers. Often they filled the shop and spilled out on to the pavement. Ordinary customers, old men coming for their tobacco and old ladies doing their bits of shopping, had to push their way through the throng. Younger ladies didn't seem to mind the crush and enjoyed the jokes I didn't understand.

All the young local men were away, in uniforms, drinking tea and getting shot at some place else.

One day, the scream of a falling bomb sent everyone in the shop diving into a heap on the floor. Tea everywhere. The house of Mr Lang, the chemist just up the road, was destroyed.

We had no garden. The tiny yard at the back was filled with sacks of potatoes, carrots and turnips. Even our big tin bath on the coal bunker was full of cabbages and cauliflowers from one Saturday bath night to the next.

The shop, then, was the playground of my toddler years. That the shop was perpetually full of soldiers and sailors seemed quite normal to me. In 1940 the whole world seemed full of soldiers and sailors. It was fun crawling in and out of their legs, while they stood among the sacks of veg and drank tea and joked. It was educational too. I learned very colourful language. This I directed at any approaching old lady's legs.

The men decided this child needed discipline. I was drilled every morning. Dressed either as a soldier or sailor, depending on who was to be Drill Sergeant, I was inspected in the shop, then marched up and down the pavement while massed ranks of tea drinkers shouted, 'Left Right, Left Right, About Turn, Pick Them Feet Up!'

Our loo was in the back yard, and there was a bus stop next to the wall of the loo. The Number 4 bus arrived at that stop every thirty minutes, but the queue of people started forming long before the bus was due. I hated going to the loo with a queue of locals chatting just the other side of the wall, especially if I thought I was going to be noisy (during the pea season for instance). I used to try to time it so that I was doing my business just as the engine of the bus was thundering away and the conductor was shouting, 'Move along inside, please.'

More than sixty thousand sailors moved into Lowestoft as the naval base grew. The base was sited in a little wooded park called Sparrow's Nest. All it had was a small concert hall, a thatched cottage, an open-air bandstand and a goldfish pond. There were no barracks, so all the sailors had to be accommodated in boarding houses and any spare rooms around the district. The town was choked with sailors, in fact they were told to walk along the sea front rather than block the main street. Adding to the congestion were the thousands of soldiers who did their final assault training along the cliffs before going overseas. As well as the British troops there were Free French, Poles and Czechs. Almost every household had uniformed lodgers.

Thousands of sailors strolling along the sea front was too good a target to miss, and there were many dive bomber raids.

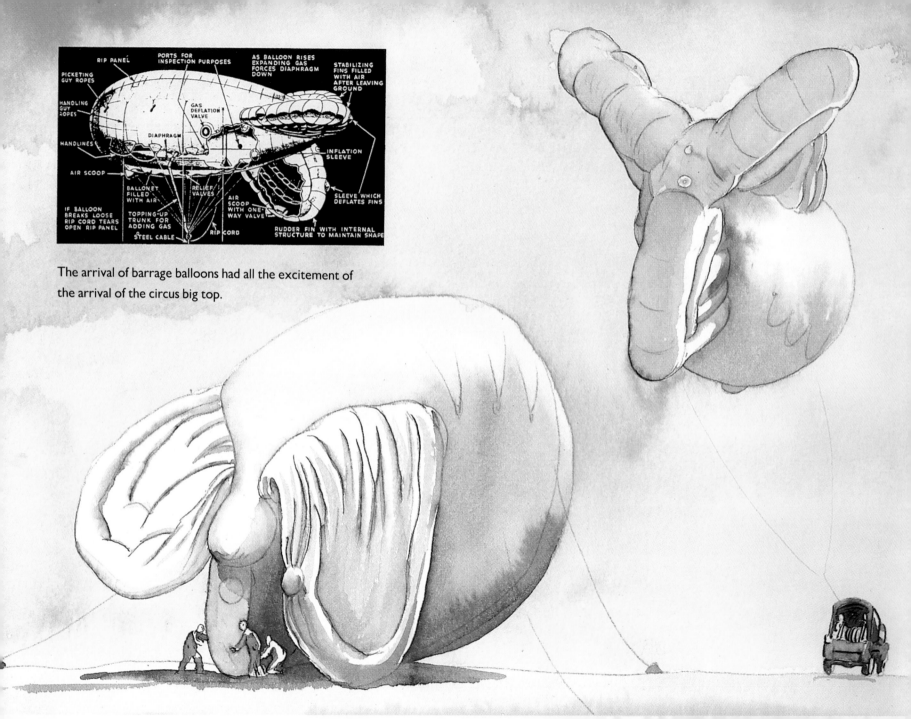

PICKETING
GUY ROPES

RIP PANEL

PORTS FOR
INSPECTION PURPOSES

AS BALLOON RISES
EXPANDING GAS
FORCES DIAPHRAGM
DOWN

STABILIZING
FINS FILLED
WITH AIR
AFTER LEAVING
GROUND

HANDLING
GUY ROPES

GAS DEFLATION
VALVE

HANDLINES

DIAPHRAGM

AIR SCOOP

INFLATION
SLEEVE

IF BALLOON
BREAKS LOOSE
RIP CORD TEARS
OPEN RIP PANEL

BALLONET
FILLED
WITH AIR

TOPPING-UP
TRUNK FOR
ADDING GAS

RELIEF
VALVES

AIR
SCOOP
WITH ONE-
WAY VALVE

SLEEVE WHICH
DEFLATES FINS

STEEL CABLE

RIP CORD

RUDDER FIN WITH INTERNAL
STRUCTURE TO MAINTAIN SHAPE

The arrival of barrage balloons had all the excitement of
the arrival of the circus big top.

The extra member of our household was Aunt Louie. Her husband died about the same time as my father. She came to help my mother and was a powerful force around the place. She did everything with gusto. Her laughter stopped traffic.

On Mondays the scullery would be full of steaming washing, with the huge copper boiling away, Aunt Louie winding the wheel of the old mangle, and the bleached wooden rollers spurting rainbows through clouds of steam.

The scullery was also where the teas were made, so mother was back and forth through this pandemonium with cups and saucers. The big black kettle added its puffs to the huffing and puffing of Aunt Louie as she sang along to the radio. It was like living in a very active volcano.

Mum and Aunt Louie were a good team. They had a wonderful way with the legions of men who, for a brief moment in the tumult of their lives, found a cup of tea, a cigarette and a chat at the corner shop.

Some stayed longer. Some formed friendships which continue still. But for many of them our substitute family was to be the last family they would know.

Even today Aunt Louie cries when she talks about 'all those lovely boys'. And then, drying her eyes, she says, 'Oh, but we had the time of our lives.' Certainly the air was rich with jokes and banter, no doubt bawdy much of the time. It would come rippling up the stairs as I slipped into sleep.

Wash Day (Painted 1951)

The long, the short and the tall engaged in endless card games. Len, tall, thin and ginger; Darkie, Lofty, Dusty, Pop; and Adam, killed in Burma aged just nineteen.

One particular friend of Mum and Aunt Louie was a big sailor from Mevagissy called Pop. He used to fill my head with tales of Cornwall, a land full of smugglers and seas full of shipwrecks.

One day, Pop took me out for the day to Beccles. We rowed about on the river, and he showed me how to put a worm on a hook and then I fell in. It would have been against naval regulations for Pop to part with any of his uniform, so I rode home on the bus in his giant vest.

Worse was to follow. A few days later, 'Aunt Tishie' (like many of my Aunts, she was not even remotely related) took me to her house for dinner and a run in the fields.

Sitting at the dinner table I was too shy to ask to go to the loo – and pooed in my pants. When her nose told her what had happened she washed me down in the copper and dressed me in a pair of enormous bloomers. She then marched me home and into the shop, past massed ranks of tea drinkers, to a chorus of 'Left Right, Left Right!' and 'Wot uniform do you call that, Sergeant Major?'

There was no shortage of uniformed knees to sit on in the evenings. Soldiers and sailors were billeted in most of the houses round about, and my Mum's front room was a favourite place for a card school. They sat round the table under a cloud of smoke. They couldn't get their knees under the table because, of course, that space was occupied by boxes of powdered milk, as were all corners of the room.

They loved to come to parties. At one of my birthday parties, Gus the sergeant had fallen asleep on the settee with a cigarette in his hand. All the children sat and watched as the butt burned down to the flesh.

Christmas night, 1942, I remember looking back into the room as Mother carried me to the stairs. A sea of faces in the smoke. They were dressed as soldiers and sailors but wearing paper hats. Other boys' fathers, sitting round our table wishing it was their little boy they had just kissed goodnight.

A village shop window, stuffed full, with nothing costing more than a penny (you could ask for a penn'orth of anything) is a sight no child can pass. The children of Pakefield were poor. A penny to spend was a rare treat. The spending required a lot of thought and took a lot of time. The penny was spent many times over in the imagination as they peered over the boxes of veg outside the shop at the rows of glass jars at the back of the window.

Pear drops, humbugs, fruit drops, liquorice comforts, gob-stoppers. You got more pear drops for a penny, but you might have to share them with your little brother or sister, or any of the notorious *Botwright* brothers if you happened to meet one in a back opening. Gob-stoppers last longer and you were less likely to have to share (although half-sucked gob-stoppers were often passed round, usually from my pocket and then mouth to mouth through the Botwright hierarchy).

Liquorice comforts were most fun. They were sucked slowly until only the black centre remained. This stained all your teeth black. If you were careful you could blacken only a few, or every other one. Earlier in the sucking stage, while there was still colour on the comforts, you could war-paint yourself and several other members of the gang in the full range of candy colours. Psychedelia came early to the Hill Green Gang.

Now, it was my good fortune, as a toddler, to be placed in the middle of this Aladdin's Cave of penny treasures. The only place safe from the feet of busmen and the Allies, and where my mother could keep an eye on me, was in the shop window. Also, away from the dark threat of their skirts, I was less likely to be rude to old ladies.

This was my window on the world. A window criss-crossed with anti-blast sticky tape, but a window which burnt penny-sized holes in the pockets of children in the street. A window past which swirled the machinery of war, the baker's horse-drawn van, the brewers' drays, and Stewey White, the tipsy coalman whose horse took him home every night.

Every ten minutes or so a bus crew would arrive for their five-minute tea break. They liked it 'hot 'n' strong'.

At one end of the glass counter was a big wooden bakers' tray, full of very dull-looking cakes. Some had a fingerprint of jam on top to suggest memories of a cherry. Others had a little black currant on top. If you saw a cake with two currants, one of them would be a fly.

Sitting in the shop window in summer was not without danger. Any bruised fruit attracted swarms of wasps. The wasps would gorge themselves for a while, then climb with sticky feet part way up the window and doze off in the sun. Boys outside the window would pretend to lick them off, or drum on the glass with their fingers and stir the wasps up into such a fury that they would dive-bomb the closely packed tea-swilling customers.

I don't think I was ever stung, despite having the stickiest face and fingers in the village.

THE K.O.S.B.'S

The King's Own Scottish Borderers manned positions around the district, and Company D was billeted in Pakefield School and a large cottage next door called Rookery Nook. Many were in tents in the garden.

The men of Company D were a particularly friendly lot, and Gus Dalgliesh had a miniature uniform made for me. I was inspected each morning in the shop, and any dullness of button or smudge of chalk on the chequered capband was duly noted. Apparently I took all this very seriously, and was particularly spick and span each time Company D marched past on church parade.

On one occasion a crowd of King's Own Scottish Borderers were in the bar of the Tramway pub, opposite our shop, when a pack of raiders suddenly dived and machine-gunned the street. The KOSBs and other customers hit the floor, and the only casualties were two or three pints on the mantelpiece above the fire. Two other KOSB lads were less fortunate. They were taking a dixie of tea around to comrades in the positions when the raiders attacked. They dropped the tea and dived for cover. They landed head first in a pigsty owned by an old character known as 'Pigmalion'. They were not warmly welcomed when they finally arrived with the tea.

Talking of smells, the soldiers used to raid the nearby pea fields when they felt hungry. They would eat their fill, then stuff their kitbags to share with their mates. Queer noises were heard through the night, caused by what they called 'musical fruit'.

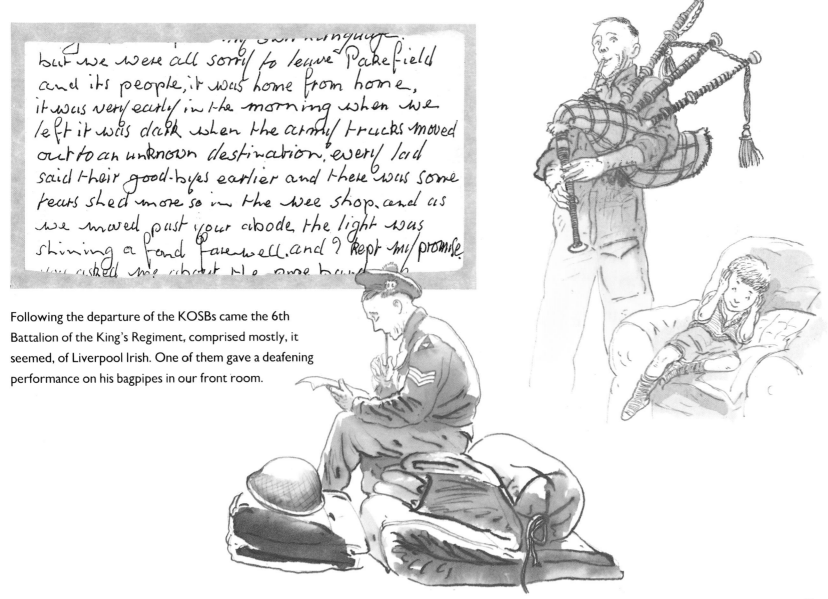

but we were all sorry to leave Pakefield
and its people, it was home from home,
it was very early in the morning when we
left it was dark when the army trucks moved
out to an unknown destination. every lad
said their good-byes earlier and there was some
tears shed more so in the wee shop. and as
we moved past your abode, the light was
shining a fond farewell. and I kept my promise.

Following the departure of the KOSBs came the 6th
Battalion of the King's Regiment, comprised mostly, it
seemed, of Liverpool Irish. One of them gave a deafening
performance on his bagpipes in our front room.

THE HILL GREEN GANG

As I got older, my world stretched along the London road to Hill Green. Why it was called Hill Green is a mystery. It was just the opposite. It was a hole in the ground, an old gravel pit.

At the bottom of the pit squatted the communal air-raid shelter. This was a huge square grassy mound, with air vents on top, and a flight of concrete steps descending into the dark mouth. A chilling place, frequently swilling with water, the wooden duck-boards bobbing about like life-rafts.

Local families, those without their own shelters, or who felt safer under the thick covering of concrete and earth, descended the steps in the evening, bringing their bedding in prams and wheelbarrows. Elderly people, particularly those living on their own, liked the company, and perhaps felt there was safety in numbers.

I never went there at night. We had our trusty Anderson and Morrison shelters, and the pantry under the stairs where Pud and Ivan slept.

In the daytime, the Hill Green shelter became our favourite place to play. Its grassy slopes, covered in spring and summer with wild flowers, were Wild West mountains from which we could swoop down on to the plains and attack Brenda Smith and the other 'settlers' playing 'house' in the abandoned Builders' Yard.

Most of my friends lived in the roads bordering Hill Green. It was our territory. Children from other districts strayed there at their peril.

Once we caught the leader of the Ship Road Gang, who was called 'Woof'. He was tied to a ladder and smoked over a damp fire on the steps of the shelter. I don't remember if Woof was supposed to be a German or a Cowboy.

For some reason, we always liked to be the Indians. Cowboys were so clean and broke into songs and yodels. Also, we wanted to be the pirates, the smugglers, the highwaymen, the cut-throats every time, and never the 'goodies'.

Of course we played 'British and Germans' from time to time, but no one would 'be' the Germans, so we couldn't indulge in the hand-to-hand grappling that we enjoyed. We had to be satisfied with long-range sniping at imaginary foes or a passing old lady. 'Dive bombing', with arms outspread, thumbs firing and engine screaming, was a favourite with us and very unpopular with old ladies. But none of us would ever 'be' the Germans.

The Hill Green shelter was also used in the real war for manoeuvres. A position to be surrounded, scaled and taken by wave after wave of soldiers in training. From a trench next to the little field where the baker kept his van horse, the troops crept in various formations towards the 'enemy stronghold'. Sometimes there were thunder flashes and smoke bombs to add to the drama.

At other times, motorcycle dispatch riders (male and female) came there for training, and careered up and down the slopes, wheels spinning and mud flying. I remember one bike bouncing down the slope and bursting into flames.

Motorcycle side-car combinations, with a gun mounted on the side-car, also roared and slithered over our Hill Green.

They would come and go, the soldiers. This battalion, that battalion. We knew all their badges and where they were from. But we, like them, never knew where they were going.

RAIDERS

Because of the nearness of the town to enemy airfields, usually there was no warning of attack – just a roaring engine from low cloud, a couple of loud 'crumps' and a hail of machine-gun fire. It was all over in seconds. Then, as the dust began to settle and the raider was escaping back over the North Sea, the warning wail of the siren would begin. This could be repeated several times in a day, or there might be a lull for a week or more.

Rainy, misty mornings were the times of greatest fear. Lowestoft's worst raid was on a day of snow, just before dusk. One lone raider loomed out of cloud above the main street and dropped four bombs on to shops and a crowded restaurant.

Seventy people were killed and more than a hundred injured. The individual dive-bomber made it seem much more personal – one enemy plane looking for someone to kill.

Opposite the Green was the Fire Station. Exhausted fire crews, sitting on the gleaming red engines, watched the war games on the Green.

Some London firemen were sent to Lowestoft for a rest from the Blitz. They found the frequent, unpredictable hit-and-run raids of the east coast even more exhausting.

The first alarm was sounded at 11.02 a.m. on the first day of the war, Sunday, 3 September 1939; the last on Monday, 30 April 1945. The 'alert' was sounded 2,047 times, with 112 warnings in August 1940 alone.

One afternoon we children were mucking about with a football on the recreation ground, or 'Rec', as we called it. Jack, the oldest of the Botwright brothers, shouted 'Fokkers!' We ran like rabbits for the slip trenches under the trees. Twelve Fokker Wulfes swooped out of the sky without warning and flew the whole length of the town spraying cannon shells. They dropped their bombs at the north end. The back of our house was riddled with cannon fire.

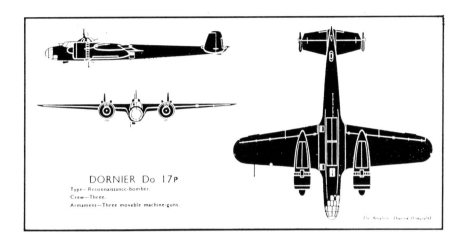

DORNIER Do 17P
Type—Reconnaissance-bomber.
Crew—Three.
Armament—Three movable machine-guns.

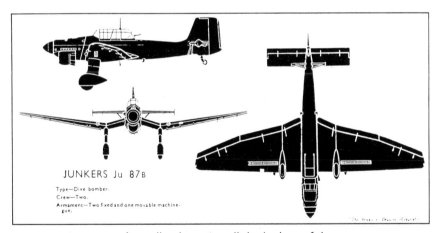

JUNKERS Ju 87B
Type—Dive bomber.
Crew—Two.
Armament—Two fixed and one movable machine-gun.

As well as knowing all the badges of the army, we children knew all the shapes and sounds of aircraft. Especially enemy aircraft. Although the fields and woods teamed with butterflies and birds, our skies and minds were full of planes.

At night Dorniers, Heinkels and Junkers, in packs of hundreds, droned over our heads for the industrial heart of the Midlands. But they did not all pass over. Sometimes one or two planes, perhaps with sick engines, dumped their load on the first town they reached.

The Borough Surveyor said in 1944 that 125 per cent of houses in the area had been either damaged or destroyed. This meant that some were damaged twice and some three times.

There were narrow escapes. Brother Pud arrived home early from school one day to say it had been bombed. A lone enemy aircraft had swooped down, almost hitting the school, climbed and circled and dropped three high explosive bombs. It was a sunny lunchtime, and Pud and his friends were playing by a corrugated iron fence in the playground. Although blown down by the bomb, the fence deflected enough of the blast to save the children. The school was wrecked. No one was seriously injured at the school, but people were killed elsewhere in the village.

Two hundred bombs dropped in fields nearby, and a partridge died of shock. A high explosive bomb fell on a garden plot and blew away a chicken house. A nearby chicken house was left with only one wall standing, but the birds were found sitting on their usual perches.

Friends struggled from their shelter to find their home a pile of bricks, but managed to rescue their canary, still singing in its battered cage.

One result of the bombing was that millions of seeds would be blown out of gardens and showered around the district. The following spring and summer, piles of rubble burst into bloom. Marigolds, irises and, best of all, potatoes sprouted everywhere.

FRIENDS AND LOCALS

One of my boyhood friends was aptly named 'Squirt'. He was small and the son of a fireman. He had a fireman's axe, the next best thing to a tomahawk. Another friend was 'Wimps'. Although a member of the Ship Road gang, he was admired for eating horse dung, in the road, for a bet.

The main London Road ran along one side of the Green and was very busy, both with local traffic and the traffic of war. But the two small roads forming the other two sides of the Green were virtually unused by motor traffic, and only the occasional bike interrupted our games of street football. We played a kind of street tennis with our feet. Sometimes passing sailors or off-duty soldiers would join in and it would be several minutes before we got our ball back.

One of the small side roads trailed off into an unpaved lane full of dips and puddles known as 'the Bumps'. It divided Hill Green from a small dense wood and was the scene of many an ambush and highway robbery.

Our trails criss-crossed the landscape of childhood. We galloped Indian file through sage brush and tumble weed, one hand holding an invisible rein and the other slapping the seat of our trousers.

Front doors were rarely opened, except to scrub the front step. The bike was out the back, and the back openings – the narrow lanes between the back-to-back houses – were the main thoroughfares. Nobody I knew had a car. We had no car, but we did have a piano as an ornament and a camera with no film.

Each back opening was lined with tremendously high 'linen posts' carrying the clothes lines. They were as high as ships' masts. They *were* ships' masts, with ships on top. The little fleet sailed the high seas above the billowing laundry. The sheds in the back yards were where we played on rainy days. Brenda Smith and the girls were always trying to put on back-yard musicals.

A billy-goat escaped during an air raid, and we chased it into our maze of back openings. It then decided to chase *us* – in and out of backyards, biting chunks out of the hanging washing. It eventually cornered Kenny and started eating his hair. Various mums with brooms rescued Kenny and we drove the goat into the field where the fishing nets were tanned and hung out to dry. The goat was then netted as if he were a tiger. By the time the farmer arrived, his goat had eaten his way out of the net but, appetite aroused, had started on a whole line of drying nets.

Of course, living in the shop, I was luckier than my friends when it came to treats. I didn't need a penny, and I didn't need to press my nose to the outside of the window and ponder the merits of sherbet lemons over barley sugar. As a toddler, I could help myself to a packet of sweet cigarettes and get a 'light' off a sailor. When I was a little older a sailor gave me a puff of a real cigarette, and I haven't tried a cigarette since.

From the age of about five, we used to smoke a weed called Tramps' Delight. It was a tall plant with thin curly leaves. When they had been dried, we rolled them in strips of newspaper, or stuffed them into home-made pipes fashioned from 'pipe wood' trees. Dried hawthorn leaves were plentiful but not so good.

From time to time we had the treat of a real tramp on our patch. They usually set up a little camp on the 'bumps' beside the wood. No doubt they were suspicious of us children, but we were usually granted an audience if we were respectful enough, and waited until invited to the fireside.

The tramp would tell us a few tall stories of the world. None of us children had been much further than the next village. Even the soldiers, the airmen and most of the young sailors, recently called up, had experience only of their home town or village. But a tramp, a 'King of the Road', could have been everywhere, and frequently told us he had. After bringing him bits of food from home, we watched and learned how to set up a fire safely, cook a pot of stew and spit with unerring accuracy on to the bobbing lid of the black boiling kettle.

Another teller of tall tales was an old fisherman we called Father Christmas because of his long white whiskers. He told tales of his cabin boy days on the great clippers and sailing ships.

On his first voyage he got homesick and jumped ship in Falmouth, the last stop before Rio. He hitched and worked his way through Cornwall and all the way home to Lowestoft. This was the first I had heard of Cornwall. He described it as a land of rocks and shipwrecks. Later, 'Pop' the sailor would tell me more. But I was already hooked.

Now, every time I drive over desolate Bodmin Moor towards my studio at St Ives, I think of the cabin boy hitching home to Suffolk.

Brother Pud, although still a schoolboy, was a very keen fisherman, and one of the old longshoremen, Alan Page or 'Pagey', took him under his wing and taught him all he knew.

'Pagey' developed a special understanding with the Commanding Officer of the large Czech Force stationed along the cliff, and eventually the longshore fishermen were allowed to venture through a secret gap in the defences and fish. They needed special permits and had to inform the authorities if they intended fishing after dark. Occasionally some would be arrested for getting back late after being unable to resist one more haul in the fading light.

'Pagey' and the Czech Commander were an incongruous couple but saluted one another with obvious respect. 'Pagey' used his rowing boat to tow and position the target for the long-range guns inland at Mutford. Thanks to his knowledge of tide and current, and spotters on the cliff top radioing range and trajectory, the gunners lobbed shells over the fields and villages to land more or less on target offshore.

The Czechs were particularly keen on fishing and were happy to help with hauling boats and cleaning nets. When a seal was seen eating the cod off the fishermen's long lines, the army put two sharpshooters into Page's boat to shoot it.

Pud and the other fishermen were also granted extra rations of cheese for their sandwiches, as the fish they caught were a valued addition to the local diet. They also received extra clothing coupons for rubber boots.

Rubber boots were hard to come by, and used to be heavily patched. When a landing craft got into difficulties, all the men were taken off and it eventually ran aground along Pakefield beach. Billy Trip, out fishing at the time, was first aboard the stricken vessel and, local hero that he was, pinched a pair of wellies. When he got them home he found they were both left feet.

On another occasion 'Pagey' found a stray mine on the shore. He put it in his wheelbarrow and took it to the Police Station. It could have blown up half of Pakefield.

'Father Time' was another old character around the village. A veteran of the First World war, he was a rather elderly Special Constable during the Second. He was suspicious of the telephone, and usually asked our mother to make his reports from the public phone box on 'the corner'. He helped in the shop from time to time, humping sacks of potatoes from the back yard to the front, and telling the troops they didn't know what a 'real' war was.

Another character who was always popping into the shop was Sid, the man from the Co-op who bought warts. He bought mine for sixpence. He gave me sixpence and my warts disappeared. He had a clubfoot. I imagined his boot full of all the warts of the village.

THE YANKS ARE COMING

Late in 1942 the traffic past our shop began to include
trucks and jeeps of the USAAF. We used to run behind
the trucks full of waving men and shout 'Got any gum
chum?' We were usually showered with packets of
chewing gum and biscuits.

They spoke like heroes. They all sounded like cowboys. (In fact, James Stewart was a flyer at a nearby base.) I dreamed that if I ran behind enough trucks they would spot me as the new Mickey Rooney and we would all go to Hollywood.

Hundreds of huge Flying Fortresses and Liberators would leave their bases in the farmlands behind Lowestoft and fill the sky like a giant iron net and thunder off toward Germany. When they came back there would be many gaps in the net. Some would return late and low, badly shot up and trying to keep out of the icy sea.

In the evenings they were determined to enjoy themselves. Some of my friends had big sisters, so they got to know the Yanks well.

From trees outside the Lowestoft Palais de Dance we could watch them jitterbugging, and sing along with the crooner. I decided to play a trumpet in a swing band instead of going to Hollywood.

SCHOOLDAYS

Around 1942 the local school was re-opened. The male
teachers were all away in the war, so we were taught by
ladies, many of them elderly. The only man in the school
was the Headmaster. His wife taught the top class, and
the big boys told us little ones horror stories of the
punishments she gave them.

The oldest teacher was Miss West, who, we all
thought, must be at least a hundred. She taught the
youngest children. She was tiny and dressed from top to
bottom in grey and lavender. I should say top to toe,
because when she swung herself up on to her high stool
we got a glimpse of her long drawers, held by elastic
below the knee. Sometimes they were a startling
periwinkle blue.

Eventually, she noticed our interest and, occasionally,
would hoist her hem demurely and say, 'The colour
today, children, is blue' (or bottle green or whatever).
Then she swung herself up on to her stool and the day
would begin.

Apart from the Headmaster and his horror wife, the
teachers were kind. However, Miss Burgess was
provoked into mass punishments when she returned to
the classroom to find us goose-stepping around and doing
the Nazi salute.

'How dare you! How dare you when your fathers are
away fighting Hitler!'

It was the usual wooden ruler on the palm of the hand.
Probably just two strokes apiece.

There were many alarms. Some false, some real and some late.

Just the threat of being sent to the Headmaster was usually sufficient to stop us getting out of hand, but towards the end of the war, a dozen of us were finally sent to his office.

We had decided to help a squad of Italian prisoners of war demolish and move the rubble of our old air-raid shelters. We used some of the bricks to bomb litter baskets hung around the walls of the playground – and caused more damage than the Luftwaffe.

We were kept quaking in the corridor for ages until all the other children had gone home. We were sure to be taken down to his wife's torture chamber. What actually happened, I don't remember. Perhaps it was so horrific I have blotted it from my memory. But probably it was just the old ruler again.

For years afterwards, when I delivered Sunday papers to the Headmaster and his wife, I would try to float silently over their crunching gravel . . . and a chill would come from their letter-box.

As the war dragged on, prisoners of war became a familiar sight and were a useful force on the farms. The Italians in particular were always ready for a game of football. Some married local girls. Our cousin Gwen married a German P.O.W. (After the war they came on a visit in a Messerschmitt bubble car.)

LIFE'S EARLY DISAPPOINTMENTS

My favourite delivery man was Charlie McCarthy with his
fruit and veg truck. Toward the end of the war, as more
convoys of ships got through, the fruit in Charlie's truck
became more exotic. An occasional barrel of grapes
packed in cork chippings was like a lucky dip. I liked to dig
my fingers down through the cork and pull out big
bunches of grapes smelling of overseas.

Then, at last, came the great day when the first long
banana box was slid from the truck on to Charlie's
shoulders, and into the shop. A space was hurriedly
cleared on the floor. The lid, which must have been about
five feet long, was prised off with a claw hammer. But
inside, instead of the five foot long banana I expected,
were rows of little yellow hands with green fingertips.

It was an anti-climax equalled only by my first visit to the pictures. When the threat of air raids was thought to be over, Pop, the sailor, took me to the Odeon. We went to see John Wayne in *Stage Coach*. Sitting in the dark was thrilling. At the far end of the darkness was Mexico, all orange and yellow, a flight of white steps with deep blue shadows leading to an arch with red roof tiles. There was green cactus and a volcano in the background.
I waited for John Wayne to gallop down the steps.

A man played a few rousing tunes on the organ, then the blazing colours of Mexico disappeared slowly up into the darkness to reveal a little flickering black-and-white screen behind. All the movement and noise and Indians couldn't make up for the lost promise of Mexico. The best bit of the film was the strange curly black hair that twirled and vibrated in the corner of every scene. Sometimes it suddenly uncurled and lashed across the screen like a serpent.

FARM DAYS

An old single-decker bus took us over the Dam and across the marshes. We got off the bus at the rise of the hill, before the beech wood. The Ruthern's cottage on the farm's land stood in the shade of a giant pear tree. In front of the cottage was the old well, smelling of mossy brick and deep cool water.

From there, the land sloped to the water meadows and marshes and on eventually to the grey sea. Always grey, even in high summer, This low land was criss-crossed with dikes, thick with bullrushes and alive with sticklebacks and dragonflies.

Great variety of grasses. Some perfect for picking your teeth, some for whistles, some for making rude noises, some for darts, and some for looping into a noose which,

when pulled tight, catapults the head of the grass like a cannon ball. The white trumpets of bindweed were great for catching bees.

All seen close-up as we slithered commando-style, faces camouflaged with mud, bullrush bayonets bristling at the end of their green barrels.

We were savages, chasing rabbits with knobbly sticks.
Their last refuge was the dwindling rectangle of standing
corn – a golden citadel about to fall.

One time, a girl named Hazel stayed at the farm. We called her Hy Hazel after the actress. She was a bit posh and used to lean out of her bedroom window brushing her hair like Rapunzel and teasing us boys.

I remember taking her down through the beech wood to meet the old couple who lived in a little cottage with their grown-up son. The son was a bit 'slow' but wonderful with birds and animals.

The Americans gave him a real jeep without wheels. They parked it outside his gate by the road. The two of us, the grown 'slow' man and me, aged six, used to spend hours chasing Germans in a jeep with no wheels.

At the end of a day a special pleasure was hauling water from the well. A whirl of the iron handle sent the bucket hurtling down to strike the water like a dead bell. It would sink with a couple of lurches. Then the struggle of winding it up, the bucket swinging slowly dropping diamonds in the dark.

Then into the cottage for Mrs Ruthern's rabbit pie. The crust thick and golden and dark brown round the edges. Steam poured from the white funnel in the centre, and more steam when the knife went in, and the smell of carrots and onions. The first big triangle went to Mr Ruthern's plate with a mountain of potatoes from the garden. There was milk from the cows, water from the well. Everything else came from the garden. Currants and gooseberries, and delicious cooking apples. Pears hard as flint, and small, soft yellow ones. All kinds of plums and greengages and strange and wonderful varieties of apple.

Mr Ruthern cut the bruises off the windfalls with his clasp knife and ate the slices off the blade. From time to time he would stretch over the table toward me and I loved to take the slice from the blade. His hand and forearm were nut brown, but when he stretched and his sleeve slid up, his arm was startlingly white.

After the meal he would make sure his old gun was clean and put it away high out of reach, then doze off, his feet on a sleeping dog.

A RELIGIOUS EXPERIENCE

First day at Sunday school, six years old. Eight-year-old John Moore arrives red with excitement.

'You should see the apples,' he whispered. 'Millions of them. Easy. Just down the lane from here. Get over the fence easy.'

Tom and Billy Botwright, eyes shining, nod.

'Yeh, on our way home.'

The hot sunny afternoon, the droning vicar, the little pictures we were given to look at, the Lord's Prayer, full of words I didn't know the meaning of, and all the time my head full of apples and fences and fear.

Billy Botwright was my classmate, and tough, and I valued his friendship. I would do anything not to appear chicken in his eyes. Anything he would do, I would do.

The fence was bigger than I expected, and I couldn't see any apples at first. John Moore pointed out a few shrivelled little green ones at the tops of high branches. (My mother had a shop full of apples. Why was I trying to pinch these?) Around the trees was a quagmire liberally covered with chicken droppings. The chickens were as ominous as vultures.

Billy Botwright was first over the gate. We followed in a heap. By the time we reached the trees our boots were covered in so much slippery goo that climbing the trees was impossible.

Suddenly, the sunny Sunday afternoon was blotted out by a shape all black and Dracula. The Vengeance of the Lord – the Vicar defending his shrivelled cookers – had me by the throat.

The Botwrights had disappeared. John Moore was dropping to freedom from the top of the fence.

'Come back,' yelled the Vicar, Strather Hunt, 'I know who you are.'

'No fear!'

The Vicar pointed to a notice – Trespassers will be Prosecuted.

I was marched into the ghostly porch of the vicarage – not inside, because of the state of my boots.

'What's your name?' he asked through his fangs. I hoped there was a strong chain attached to his dog collar.

He knew who I was, so I told him.

'And who were the others?' Ah, my chance to be brave. Actually, I was too scared of Billy Botwright to ever tell on him.

The next day the village policeman, PC 'Pal' Whiteman arrived at our door. I hid under the front room table, and my mother said I was out. I heard PC Pal laugh and say something about 'as we forgive them who trespass against us'.

I should have paid more attention to the Lord's Prayer. So should have the Vicar.

DOODLEBUG!

The summer of 1944 saw the first 'doodlebugs'. Shaped like a plane but with no pilot, the doodlebug had a jet engine and fell to earth when the fuel ran out. They were aimed at London, but nine out of ten were shot down before they crossed the coast. Some were 'winged' and went off on an erratic course over the town. Local people flocked to the cliff-tops each evening to see the spectacular show as the doodlebugs came over the horizon to be met by the barrage of the coastal guns (now largely 'manned' by ATS girls). A direct hit would result in a tremendous orange flash, a bang and a shower of shrapnel, hopefully over the sea. But a 'winged' doodlebug could slide off in any direction. If its fiery tail went out it would hit the ground in fifteen seconds.

We were standing by our back door one evening watching a doodelbug drone overhead. Suddenly its red light went out. 'It's coming down!' someone yelled, and we rushed indoors and all dived under the Morrison shelter. I banged my head on the iron frame and forgot about the explosion.

It fell a mile away, on a farm. Next morning we all went to see the damage. The farm buildings were a pile of rubble and the air was full of feathers.

The doodlebug, or V1, was followed by the V2. They came silently, at any time, over the horizon, the deadly tip of a vapour trail a hundred miles long. Fired from deep within Europe as the Allies advanced. The east coast remained within range until the bitter end.

THE END

At the end of the war in Europe, 'Father Time' assumed
responsibility for the bonfire celebrations. The
accumulated junk and rubble of the war years made not
one, but three huge heaps on Hill Green.

There was a competition for the best Hitler Guy, and
there were some Himmlers, and Goebbels and many bald
Mussolinis.

There has never been a Guy Fawkes night like it. All
three bonfires went up together. All the Hitlers and
henchmen toppled and blazed.

VJ Day was much the same. We burned Hitlers again, and a lot of yellow Guys with big teeth and glasses.

The big black-out blind from our front room window escaped the bonfires. My brothers made it into an enormous kite.

The windy day at the end of the war inspired many other kite makers. In my childhood, children's games seemed to come around in seasons. There was a time for hoops, a time for football, a time for fishing. This was the time for kites.

'It's too big. It won't fly!' shouted the boys as they held on to their kites and pushed and shoved to inspect mine. But it did fly. Such was the squabble to hold the line, however, that no one did.

It soared up over Hill Green and over the ashes of the victory bonfires, over the Fire Station and the road to London.

My eyes filled with pride and tears.

Toward the end of the day, Charlie McCarthy pulled up outside the shop.

'What have you got for us today, Charlie?' asked Mum.

He grinned and hoisted me over his shoulder and dumped me into the back of his truck. There, amongst the fruit and veg, was my big black kite.

'It dive bombed me near the Dam' Charlie said.

So it was true, all the things the grown ups had said during the dark days. Now the war was over everything would be all right, there'll be blue birds over the white cliffs, not barrage balloons. And men with rainbows on their chests would, like my kite, come home.

And the memory of those who passed through our village on the way to war will remain for ever with the ghosts of us children in the fields and woods of long ago.

Received your letter with the very sad news of your
mother's passing, and with sadness in my heart her passing
has left me with a little emptiness. But I'm honoured to
have shared in her friendliness among so many, for so
many years. She was held in high esteem by her boys who
frequented the wee shop on the corner, for their sweets,
cigs, a coffee and a wee motherly chat – and when we
have our reunion this year we will remember her.

Gus Dalgliesh KOSB, May 1982

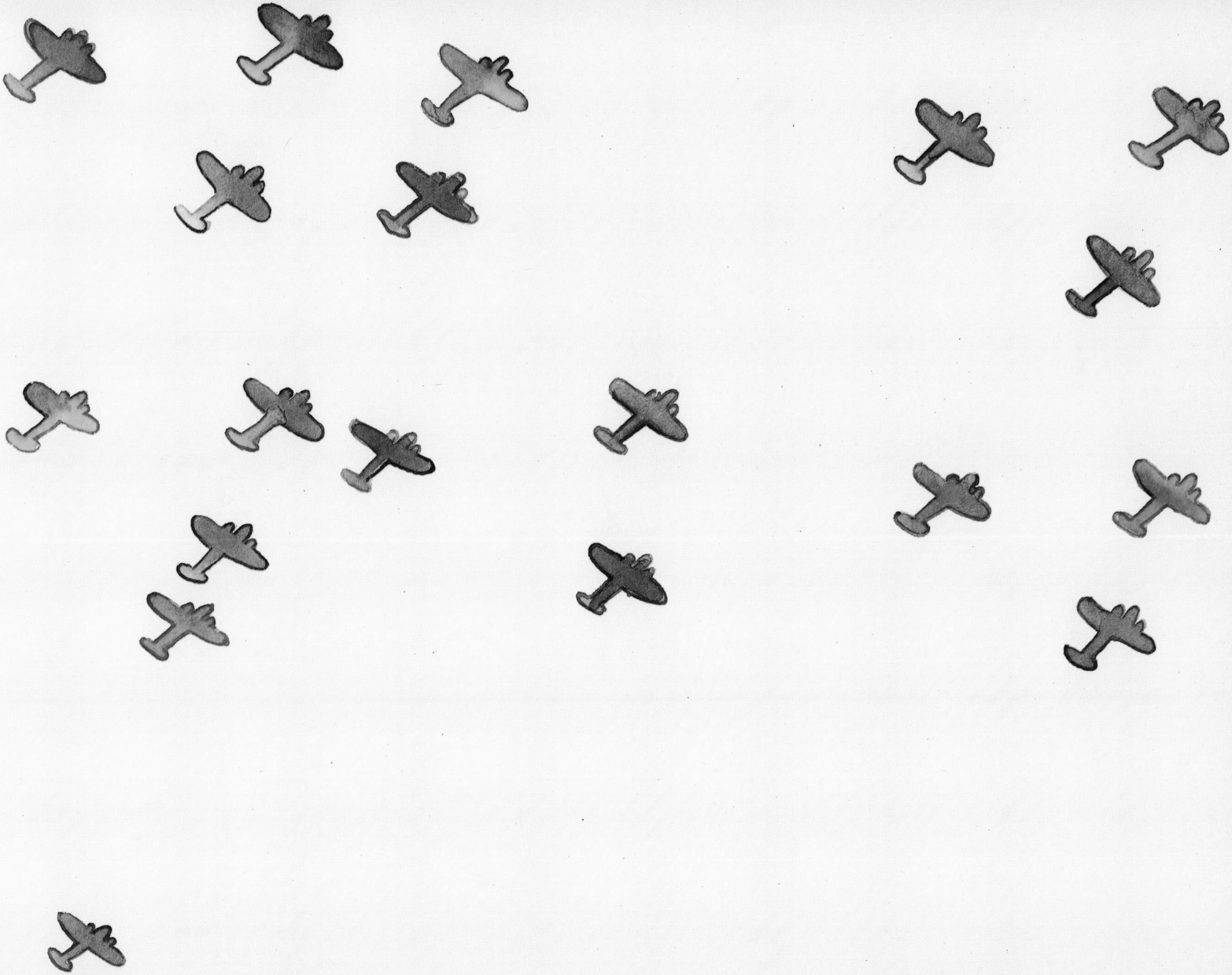

AFTER THE WAR
WAS OVER

It was summer, 1945. The war was over. The victory bonfires blazed on the village green and the embers remained hot enough for days to bake potatoes. When the fires cooled, the ashes drifted and spiralled like silver-grey snow.

The victory flags stayed up for ages. More flags and bunting were added as the men began to return home to the village. Some took months to get back from the Far East, particularly if they had been badly wounded or had suffered in Japanese prisoner-of-war camps.

102

The pain felt by the children whose fathers would never return was made worse by the flags and 'Welcome Home' banners. The last man home was Sid, from a Japanese camp.

Sid swopped his army uniform for a bus conductor's outfit and thereafter drank hot tea from the saucer with all the other bus crews in my mother's shop.

When each man was demobilized from National Service he was a given a cheap, ill-fitting 'demob' suit. These suits lasted within families for generations. They were first worn only on Sundays and at funerals and weddings. Then eventually the trousers were worn beneath dungarees for work, and the jackets passed down through the sons.

Teenagers (who were not then invented) did not have their own fashions. Children's clothes were the same as adults' clothes, but in smaller sizes. Younger brothers had the cast-offs of bigger brothers, but cut-down to fit. Not until the mid 1950s, when the Teddy Boys created their unique outfits, did the younger generation begin to have their own fashions.

The shop was also our home and it stood with two other little houses on a triangular traffic island surrounded by three roads. It was at the end of the bus route from town, and after turning the buses around, the drivers and conductors had a five-minute break. Mum made tea for them in a great big pot.

Although the war was over, there were still lots of uniforms in and out of our shop. The American Forces were still around, particularly on Saturday nights.

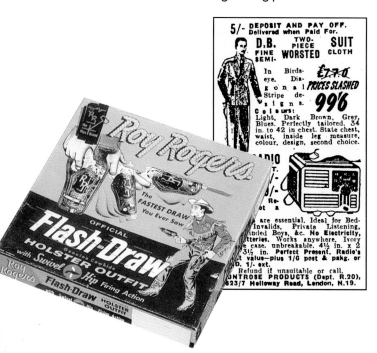

The local girls went dancing with them at the Palais de Danse, and when the Americans began to be posted home, many of the girls married them. With dreams of Hollywood shining in their eyes, they moved to isolated farm communities in the wind-blown Mid West or trailer homes on the outskirts of Texas oil towns.

The pretty sisters of some of my friends became American brides and each Christmas sent sad letters and bits of shiny Americana to their families. The twins, Arthur and Kenny, received silver six-shooters with buffalo heads carved on the handles. The rest of us boys were deeply jealous, and wished we had pretty sisters.

The landscape of war was slowly cleared. When the first small area of beach was opened up it was immediately packed with people. We children had never been on the beach before. Suddenly, there we all were.

Grannies and grandads, aunts and uncles, mums and dads, packed on to a tiny patch of beach, and beyond the wire, mile after mile of sands and shingle still stuffed with mines. Gradually the beach was cleared of mines and barbed wire.

Bren gun carriers with caterpillar tracks were used to transport the mine disposal men along the beach from the village. We used to get rides with them to the latest frontier wire, and imagine we were fighting our way across the Sahara with the Desert Rats. Then we would look through the deep slits in the blockhouse at the controlled explosions of the mines along the beach. There was a wrecked landing craft on the shore. After the mines were cleared the wreck became our pirate ship.

The final act of celebration for the end of the war was a great gathering of all the children from the area on 'The Oval' cricket ground on the foreshore below the cliffs of Lowestoft. Hundreds and hundreds of us stood in pouring rain holding bits of coloured card over our heads while the bands played.

At a given signal we had to turn the card over. Viewed from the cliffs above, where all the townspeople were gathered, the cards together formed the Union Jack and when turned over again they read 'God Save the King!' The cards went soggy and colours ran down our arms.

Back at school, it was a shock suddenly to have men as teachers. All through the war our teachers had been women, many of them rather ancient. Teaching became much louder and punishment swift and effective. However, the new young Headmaster, Mr Newson, was, I thought, a great improvement on the old Head. The retirement of the old Head also meant the end of the reign of terror of his fearsome wife who taught the top class.

One day, at school, we had a visit from a policeman. We assembled in the school hall and the policeman laid out a collection of mines on the floor. There were many shapes and sizes. We were told *never* to touch anything metal which we might find lying on the beach. It was hoped that the local beach was now completely clear, but mines could still be loose in the sea and might get washed up on the shore. The policeman then stood on a mine and the metal casing flew apart. We screamed and jumped in the air. Even the teachers gasped and closed their eyes.

Of course, the policeman's mines were harmless, empty cases, but what a shock! We would never touch a metal object found on the beach – or anywhere else for that matter.

Miss West and other teachers retired but the younger women teachers stayed on. Pat Palmer was my favourite. Sometimes she took us for P.T. When we were doing physical jerks, each time she raised her arms above her head her short, yellow jumper rose above her waist. The arc of bare flesh above her skirt was like the morning sun rising from a dark sea. It was a whole new dawn for me.

One day, Miss Palmer asked us to paint a picture of a highwayman. At the end of the session she held up my picture as a good example.

'That's not very good, Miss,' chirped one of the boys. 'The bushes are just scribbles.'

'That's what real artists do,' replied Miss Palmer. 'They don't draw every leaf. They give the *impression* of things.'

It seemed like an easy way out to me, and it was the first time I had heard of artists. Not a bad job if you can get away with scribbles.

Note the turned-down wellies. I thought they made me look like a pirate.

There was a lot of saluting of flags in those days. The big occasion was Empire Day. The whole school would assemble in the playground. Old Father Time, the caretaker, slowly and dramatically hoisted the Union Jack up the flagpole while we saluted. Then we would sing 'God Save the King', and 'Land of Hope and Glory' and various songs of Empire. After some prayers we went in to school and looked at the big map which showed most of the world coloured pink.

I assumed that pink was the colour of the Empire because British people were supposed to be pink. But I always thought it a soppy colour and in games of Cowboys and Indians always wanted to be the Indian brave, or Sabu the elephant boy.

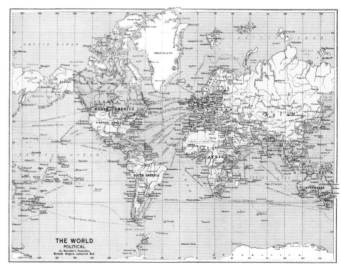

One night, just after the end of the war, my mother took us all to the Hippodrome, the local theatre.

She had often told us of a night before the war when she had gone to the Hippodrome to see Gracie Fields, 'Our Gracie'. That evening had kept our Mum and Aunt Louie in songs all through the war.

Now we were all going! I was so excited. There were lots of people on the stage at the beginning, singing and dancing in a line.

Then a lady came on in a spectacular red dress and lots of fruit on her head. She was singing and shaking about, then she took off her dress. Then her stockings. When her hands went behind her back to take off her bra, I pretended I had dropped something on the floor and ducked under my seat. I was too embarrassed to be looking at all this while sitting next to my mother.

Of course, I continued to peep from under my seat.

Suddenly the bra was off and two tennis balls dropped out, and the man (for it was an all-man show) danced off the stage, bouncing the balls. What a relief. The show was called *Soldiers In Skirts*.

Bomb sites continued to be our adventure playgrounds. Marigolds and potatoes grew in the ruins of buildings, and blitzed gardens offered apples and pears. Of course, we ate them long before they were ripe.

Some of my friends who had been bombed out of their homes were living in ex-Army huts. Geoffrey Dann, who had curly ginger hair and freckles, lived in one and I rather envied his new home with its great curved iron roof like an aircraft hangar.

R.B.1
16
MINISTRY OF FOOD
1953-1954
SERIAL No
BE 130?

RATION BOOK

Surname MACE (IVAN A Initials
Address 44 FLORENCE Rd
PAKEFIELD LOWESTOFT

IF FOUND RETURN TO ANY FOOD OFFICE

F.O. CODE No.

E–E
2

Pre-fabricated houses (prefabs) were quickly built — more than 40,000 between 1945 and 1946.

The rationing of wartime continued long into the peace Bread and potatoes for a year or two, and butter, cheese, bacon, meat, tea and sugar were all rationed until 1954. Sweets were unrationed, at last, in April 1951. But so much was instantly gobbled up that rationing was re-introduced in July.

The large gun emplacements dotted along the clifftops remained for years after the war. The 'pillboxes' and network of underground concrete tunnels can still be found beneath dense tangles of brambles and nettles.

Puggy Utton, a local hermit, lived in a pillbox and some of the connecting tunnels for years. He wore all his clothes at once: several coats, a hat over a balaclava, and through the holes in his gloves could be seen more gloves.

The clifftop setting, and the fear of suddenly bumping into the mysterious Puggy in the dark tunnels, made it a favourite playground for us boys. They were smelly places, often ankle deep in water, and we would frighten ourselves with ghostly moans and screams.

A few yards back from the cliff edge were fields of turnips, peas and potatoes. We helped ourselves to the occasional turnip and handful of potatoes, chipped them up with Squirt's fireman's axe and boiled them in a tin can for dinner. Squirt, being a fireman's son, always had a small axe and a box of matches.

We were often away from home the whole day, roaming free like a band of Indians. Parents in those days had less reason to worry about the whereabouts of their children. Everyone in the village knew everyone else. The roads were not full of strangers in cars.

The cliff path in spring and summer buzzed and shimmered with bugs and beetles and chirruping grasshoppers. There were butterflies in great numbers: Red Admirals, Painted Ladies, Orange Tips, Clouded Yellows, spectacular Peacocks and the modest Common Blue. I thought it was the most *uncommon* blue. A drop of the blue Mediterranean against the grey-brown of the North Sea.

There were lacewings and stoneflies, and dragonflies like green camouflaged bombers. As we lay in the grass, we were dive-bombed by hornets and sawflies, digger wasps and bees. Red ants and black ants surrounded and attacked us like Lilliputian armies.

If we leaned over the cliff edge we could see, just out of reach, Sand Martins constantly landing and taking off from their vertical airfield, the cliff face riddled with their nesting holes.

The cliff path wound through head-high hogweed and cow parsley. There was dockweed which we used to spit on and press on nettle stings to ease the pain. (I thought they were called 'Doc' because it was short for doctor.) May blossom hid thorns which could rip both shirt and shoulder, and nettles stung bare legs as we whooped and galloped our imaginary Indian ponies through the sage brush.

Player's Cigarettes
Gt. Britain—
Painted Lady

Player's Cigarettes
Gt. Britain—
Orange Tip

Player's Cigarettes
Gt. Britain—
Clouded Yellow

Player's Cigarettes
Gt. Britain—
Red Admiral

WILLS'S CIGARETTES.

COMMON BLUE.

WILLS'S CIGARETTES.

PURPLE EMPEROR.

In late summer, corn and poppies were laid low by harvesters and surprised blue-eyed periwinkles blinked from the fields of stubble.

We didn't appreciate the beauty of such things then. We noticed them only when our bunch of harebells, buttercups and field forget-me-nots and wild honeysuckle handed to our mums might soften our late tea-time return.

Vinca minor

PERIWINKLE

Family RANUNCULACEÆ

BUTTERCUP

Family BORAGINACEÆ

FORGET-ME-NOT

Lonicera Periclymenum

HONEYSUCKLE

Family PAPAVERACEÆ

RED POPPY

Family CAMPANULACEÆ

BELLFLOWER

Against this background of beauty, we sometimes found horror. Farmers were angered by rabbits eating their crops and introduced a disease called myxomatosis which spread through the rabbit population with great speed and with terrible results.

Often, we would turn a bend in the path and find a rabbit crouched before us. Normally, rabbits would bound away to safety, but the diseased rabbits did not move. They stared with accusing, bulging eyes in pitifully swollen heads, ears flat along quivering bodies until they died.

We were brutal little boys, and had in the past chased rabbits in the hope of getting one for the pot. But the suffering of the diseased rabbits sickened us. Even our dogs seemed horrified, and whimpered and peered at the rabbits from behind our legs.

One day, two strange boys arrived at school. One was very tall, the other had a very round face and startling white hair. The strangest thing about them was their trousers, which were incredibly short. We Pakefield boys had the usual very baggy British knee-length trousers which made the backs of your legs sore in cold, wet weather, and long grey socks which always slipped down around our ankles. These strange boys had tight trousers, hardly lower than their bums, and bright white ankle socks.

The tall boy was called Henno, and the other Rigo. They were from Estonia, and stood in the bleak playground with their backs against the wall. Their knees looked very cold. Being British children, we teased them. Maybe children everywhere are like that if they are in a crowd.

But there was something about the two strange boys which excited me. They had come from somewhere else. They had seen things we hadn't. They were refugees.

Henno and Rigo walked past our shop every morning on their way to school. I would watch for them and walk out of the shop just as they were passing and wander along to school with them. They knew little English in the beginning and so of course spoke mostly to each other as we walked. I learned that Rigo's father was captain of a cargo ship and had managed to bring Rigo and Henno and their mothers out of Estonia before the Russians made it impossible.

After a short time, Henno and his mother moved on to Canada, and Rigo and I became close friends.

Rigo's father was sailing all over the world, and Rigo and his mother lived in a flat decorated by the paintings his father did during his long voyages. I thought the paintings were brilliant. They were always of the sea, often of a small sailboat with a man, a woman and a small boy with startling white hair at the tiller.

One day Rigo and I picked blackberries together on 'Sixteen Acre', an area of thick bushes bordering on the cliffs. I gave Rigo an empty jam jar to put his blackberries in. He asked me what it was called. I said, 'a jam jar'. He fell about laughing. 'Jam jar' were the funniest words he had ever heard. He repeated them all afternoon. 'Jam jar. Jam jar. Jam jar.'

Eventually he too moved on to live in Canada. I never heard from him again. He had taught me how to count up to twenty in Estonian, and I had taught him to say 'jam jar'. Wherever he is, I hope he has a sailboat and children with startling white hair.

Shortly after the war my mother took me to London on the train. We had free tickets because my father worked on the railway before he died. He died one month before I was born. We went to see Buckingham Palace.

Buckingham Palace was disappointing because it didn't have towers and turrets and didn't look like a palace. The guards outside still wore their khaki wartime uniforms and not red tunics and busby helmets.

Next day, we had a picnic in Hyde Park. The parks of London were still full of sheep from the wartime and the sheep got most of our picnic. In the afternoon we went to Whiteley's, a big department store which was much more like a palace. Mum bought me two model soldiers. They each cost half a crown (12$^1/_2$ pence in today's money), an enormous sum, I thought. One of them, an eighteenth-century infantryman, I still have, minus his head. It is the only toy which remains from my childhood.

I remember on my birthday a couple of years later getting a set of soldiers from an aunt. A complete set. A dozen all lined up in a box. Red tunics and busbies. I was thrilled. My mother said my aunt shouldn't have spent so much money and I was too old for such things. Too old. I could feel the lights going out on my childhood.

I grew up on a diet of comics and magazines. As my mother ran the village shop, we sold almost everything, including Sunday newspapers. The comics and magazines arrived in our shop on Wednesdays, to be delivered on Sundays. This meant I could read all the comics and as many magazines as I wanted before they were delivered.

One of my favourite comics was *Film Fun* which had real film stars in the comic strips and was printed in black and white. Laurel and Hardy were always on the cover and usually ended up having a huge meal of bangers and mash on a silver dish. I also liked Desperate Dan in *The Dandy,* who ran through brick walls to get to his enormous helpings of cow-pie. Perhaps I was attracted to these stories because of food rationing.

I also liked *The Wizard, Hotspur* and *Rover,* with their longer stories of heroic boys and dogs and secret agents. Later, a new comic, *Eagle,* appeared but I didn't like it. It was not daft enough.

Some of the magazines, particularly *John Bull,* used lots of drawings. One artist specialized in wonderful crowd scenes. Crowds at race meetings, railway stations, football matches. I remember his surname was Rose, and I wish I knew more about him.

In those days biscuits were not packed in small packets as they are now. They were delivered to the shop in large tins and customers would buy half a pound or so and Mum would weigh them out into paper bags or wrap them in old newspaper. The big biscuit tins were lined with white corrugated paper and each layer of biscuits was separated by transparent greaseproof paper. The white corrugated paper was smooth on one side. I used to draw crowd scenes on the smooth side and used the greaseproof as tracing paper. The biscuit tins were about twelve inches square, so unfolded, the paper for my crowds would be four feet long.

I used to lie on the floor in front of the fire and draw for hours. We had the Daily Mirror *for the news and the* Daily Express *because I liked to copy Rupert.*

I used to copy drawings of Jane and throw them on the fire before my mother saw them.

I loved stories of space travel and never thought it would happen in my lifetime.

Rupert and the Jumping Men—30

A moment later the tiny airplane has landed and Rupert runs forward as an old friend gets out of it. "Why, surely you're the Golliwog that runs errands for Santa Claus, aren't you?" he

like Rupert of Nutwood but you're four sizes too small!" "Yes, I am Rupert," says the little bear. "I couldn't get in here while I was my right size." And he tells why he came and how the

129

My brothers, my friends and I delivered the Sunday papers. I used to walk my paper round, kicking a tennis ball along the roads, lanes and back alleys. I was becoming football mad.

For Christmas one year I was given a table football set, and after they had delivered the papers, some of the paper boys used to stay behind and we would have a table football competition in our front room and imitate the roar of the crowd.

We played football at school, and every weekend except in the cricket season. Then in the cricket season, when the evenings were long and light, we played football every weekend *and* every evening. We also played a special version of football on the concrete road by the Green. With two players on each team it was rather like foot-tennis. 'Tap Tin', our version of 'Kick the Can', conkers, hoops, kites, fishing and the making of buggies from old prams and fish boxes, filled our days to bursting.

Girls didn't feature much in our lives. We sat next to them at school, some of my friends had them as sisters, but in general they were as popular as nettles and best avoided.

Two or three girls, however, were exceptions. They used to hover around the edge of our games and occasionally join in. The girls would try to give the ball a few hefty kicks, then invariably grab the ball and run off with it. We would give chase and the football match would degenerate into a game of rugby with us all in a heap. Sometimes I was fed up because our game had been ruined, but sometimes I found it more fun than football.

Then, one day, the ladies who worked at the local laundry decided to form a rugby team to play in a charity game. I don't remember who their opponents were going to be, but the laundry wanted to play a practice match against us boys – so they could get accustomed to the rules.

Many of the ladies were enormous and none of them bothered with the rules. They thought the game was about sitting on as many small boys as possible.

Just across the road at the back of our house was the fish and chip shop. It was the favourite place to hang about in the evenings. It had a wide pavement in front, and the light, which streamed from its big steamed-up window, was bright enough to read comics by.

The owner of the chip shop was Lofty Payne. He was sports mad and on Saturdays he often took me to Norwich in his fish van to see the football. By the time I arrived home, brother Pud would have finished his bath in front of the kitchen fire and emptied it with the bucket and gone off to meet his girlfriend, Doreen.

Usually, my big brother Ivan was in the bath, having refilled it from the kettle. I would sit at the kitchen table beside the bath and have my tea and give him a full report of the match.

If I didn't go to a match, we would listen to 'Sports Report' – Ivan in the bath and me at the tea table, checking his football coupon. Then Ivan would get out, dress in his Saturday night suit, and go to the Palais de Danse. I would then get in the bath and finish my tea.

When I eat celery I always think of those Saturday nights. I don't know if it is because I always ate celery then or whether sticks of celery remind me of Ivan's legs. The tin bath, though big for me, was far too small for Ivan. He had to be a contortionist to scrub all his bits and pieces.

Mum and Aunt Louie were still busy in the shop. I would tip out half the bath water and top it up with boiling water ready for Mum. Mum closed the shop at 7.30 on Saturdays so she could be in the bath to listen to 'Saturday Night Theatre' while Louie took the dog for a walk.

Later, I discovered the jazz programme on A.F.N. (American Forces Network). This became my bathtime listening. It was the era of the big, roaring be-bop bands and was so exciting. Sometimes I pretended my lemonade bottle was a trumpet and mimed to the mirror, standing in the bath in front of the fire.

Our dog was called Sandy. We got him as a tiny puppy in the winter of 1947, the worst winter of the century. Deep snow stayed for weeks. Little could move on the roads, and the railways were at a standstill. Some power stations ran out of coal, and electricity was turned off several times a day. Farmers could not plough their fields so the following harvest was poor.

Mum, me and Sandy.

Of course, we boys loved the snow, but it was difficult for a tiny puppy like Sandy. He was too small to walk through the deep snow, so he jumped into and out of my footprints wherever we went.

Spring brought gales and floods. By 1948 rations were lower than during the war. The general feeling was that things could only get better. Very young children were given free orange juice, cod liver oil (yuk) and tonics and vitamins. Free milk was provided for all children at school until Mrs Thatcher the Milk Snatcher took it away from all children over seven in 1971.

Although many men had returned home from the Army, Navy and Air Force, many younger men were being 'called up' to take their places and maintain the 'Peace' around the world. Eighteen-year-olds were required for a compulsory period of two years' military service, so that if war broke out again Britain would have a large number of trained young men ready to fight.

Lowestoft station, like railway stations throughout the country, continued to be a place of sad farewells. Dads were home at last, but now elder brothers were in uniform and going away.

Trouble started in Palestine. Jews and Arabs were killing each other and both sides were killing the British.

Ivan was called up and sent to Egypt. We were all terribly sad to see him go, but his girlfriend Barbara, 'B', took me to the pictures every Thursday evening because she didn't like going alone.

We saw all kinds of films. Whatever was showing, we went. In addition to the main feature there would be the B film, usually a black-and-white drama. Then a cartoon or two, and the 'trailers' of forthcoming films, which always looked absolutely fantastic and the 'best film ever'. Then there would be a travelogue or short, factual film about making golf balls or knitting sweaters in the Hebrides. Sometimes there would be a singer on stage singing posh songs. Sometimes a man in a bow tie and a lady in a big frock would sing soppy songs. There would then be ice-creams and fruit drinks, and then everyone would settle back in the dense cigarette smoke, for the main feature.

'B' liked lovey-dovey films with lots of music and kissing. Once she took me out of the cinema because she was horrified by a film about war. She thought it unsuitable for me and it probably made her even more worried about Ivan.

I didn't like Saturday morning pictures with all the singing or the films made specially for kids. My mates and I went on Saturday afternoons to the real films. Hopalong Cassidy, who didn't sing, and best of all, Gabby Hayes, like a Wild West Father Christmas. Roy Rogers and Gene Autry always burst into song and we booed them. We loved all things American. All our movie heroes – cowboys, Indians, even Robin Hood and his merry men – had American accents.

My favourite films were pirate films because there was always a feast where they ate all kinds of exotic fruit, had bad table manners and a good time.

Then, out of the steam and gloom of evening, Ivan's tall shape appeared with a kitbag across his shoulders.

In his kitbag were treasures from the East, as exotic as any pirate film. Sugared almonds. Dates with nuts inside. And a bedspread with camels, palm trees and pyramids for Mum. I don't know what he brought 'B' but they stopped going out together soon after.

Ivan wrote to us and sent the occasional photograph of himself and his mates standing outside tents with the pyramids far away in the distance. Eventually we got news of his return date.

I was at the Lowestoft railway station early in the morning. We had the date but not the time of his arrival. Train after train arrived. 'B' popped in to the station during her lunch break, but no sign of Ivan.

By my tenth birthday, Mum decided it was time I had a bike. All my friends had bikes. Mum was surprised I had not pestered her for one before. She didn't know I was scared of learning to ride.

It wasn't a new bike but it had a new coat of paint and was very smart and shiny. Despite the efforts of my brothers, their girlfriends and Aunt Louie, all of whom took turns running alongside the bike holding the saddle, I fell off every time they let go.

I made excuses not to ride. I said the bike was too big. Mum had wooden blocks screwed to the pedals so I could reach them more easily, but still I refused to learn. It was pointed out to me that next year I would have to go to secondary school which would be a long way to walk. 'Well, I'll learn *then*,' I said.

At about the same time, I started going to see the football at Norwich with some of the older newspaper boys. We went on the train.

Much as I loved the thrill of football, my fondest memories are of the journey there and back, and the companionship of older boys. The steam train rattled through the flat marshland of Norfolk, casting smuts over bullrushed dykes and the sails of windmills and boats on the wide broads.

The crowds in the late 1940s and 1950s were
enormous. Even Third Division teams like Norwich
regularly attracted crowds of 30,000. The supporters
packed so tightly together that it was impossible to
move. Boys were passed hand to hand over the heads
of the crowd to the front so they could see. On one
awful occasion someone behind me peed in my pocket.
Probably a Millwall supporter.

142

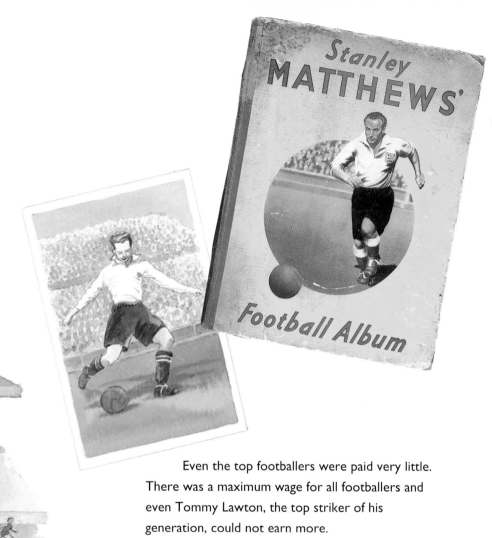

Even the top footballers were paid very little. There was a maximum wage for all footballers and even Tommy Lawton, the top striker of his generation, could not earn more.

Here is the balance sheet of Tommy Lawton's eighteen years in the game.

	£	s.	d.
40 winter weeks and 12 summer weeks at the limit for 17-year-olds	352	0	0
40 winter and 12 summer weeks at the limit for 18-year-olds	456	0	0
40 winter and 12 summer weeks at the limit for 19-year-olds	580	0	0
15 seasons on top money:			
600 winter weeks at £15 per week	9,000	0	0
180 summer weeks at £12 per week	2,160	0	0
3 benefits of £750 each	2,250	0	0
1 accrued share of benefit (three-fifths)	450	0	0
18 seasons' bonus at £1 a point (average, say, 42 points per season)	756	0	0
TOTAL	£16,004	0	0

In 1947, Denis Compton was named 'Sportsman of the Year'. He was every boy's hero because he played cricket for England and football for Arsenal and England. His face was on huge posters advertising Brylcreem. He was a dashing winger for Arsenal when they won the FA Cup in 1950. They wore gold shirts that day, and Denis looked even more glamorous than usual. His brother, Leslie, was centre half, and also kept wicket for Middlesex.

I can still name every member of that Arsenal team, as I can the Norwich team of that era, but I cannot name all the players of any team since.

BRYLCREEM

Keeps you right on top

On the side of our house was a large billboard. The posters were usually about the latest film, but sometimes there would be a giant Denis Compton smiling down above our loo.

Opposite our house, behind a row of old petrol pumps, was an even more gigantic poster of a golfer with a box of Swan Vesta matches. The two giant faces beamed at each other across the road, and in the tiny hut beside the petrol pumps Ginger Jarvis practised his trumpet, his feet sticking out through the window.

By now, Ivan and Pud were both working in the same garage in the town. Ivan was five years older than Pud, and Pud was nine years older than me. So we each had our own group of friends. I liked being with their friends – but they weren't very interested in mine.

Ivan's group all had motorbikes, and they rode around in a pack, but they couldn't be described as a motorcycle gang. In those days nobody had the flashy leather outfits bikers wear today. They didn't even have crash helmets. Just a pair of goggles, and perhaps a scarf to make them look more dashing.

Sometimes Ivan took me on the back of his bike. It was thrilling to roar along country lanes in a swarm of motorbikes and a cloud of blue smoke.

One weekend, cousin Pam came from London with a couple of girlfriends to watch their favourite speedway team, Wembley Lions, ride at Norwich. They spent Saturday with us on Pakefield beach, and Pud took them out in his boat.

It was quite a rough day, and when coming in to the shore, the boat slewed side-on to a big breaking wave and tipped everyone into the sea. The wave rolled them all up on to the beach in a tangle of arms, oars and legs, and to cheers from the local fishermen.

The three girls went to the speedway in the evening in an odd assortment of clothes borrowed from Mum and Aunt Louie. They took me with them and I was thrilled to see the legendary Tommy Price ride for Wembley. He had ridden for England many times before and after the war, and had a reputation for being a rough rider. He was booed by the Norwich fans and cheered wildly by Pam and her friends.

My favourite rider was Billy Bales. He was a local boy, and had started as a youngster on the cycle speedway track outside the stadium at Yarmouth. He was so good that he was invited to have a go on a proper speedway bike. He rode for Yarmouth Bloaters for a short time before becoming a First Division star at Norwich. The local girls loved him and the boys idolized him.

The World Champion at that time was an Australian, Jack Young, who rode for West Ham. He had great classic style, not at all like the hell-for-leather tear-aways like Tommy Price or the flashy Split Waterman.

When I went to Norwich with my mates, we always went first to the football. Then we had chips at the cattle market at the foot of Norwich Castle, before catching the bus to the speedway. On waste ground outside the stadium was the cycle speedway track — an oval scraped out of the turf and covered with cinders.

Local boys hurtled round this wearing the colours of their favourite teams. There were lots of crashes and it was always exciting. Most of the boys emulated the tactics of Tommy Price and rode their opponents off the track and into the straw bales, but they dreamed of being Billy Bales, local hero and Speedway International.

Billy Bales

After watching the cycle speedway, we had more chips, then went into the stadium. By now it was getting dark. The bright grass-green oval in the centre with the freshly painted white line around it, glowed like an atoll in a sea of volcanic ash. Men in white overalls raked the ash flat. Then with a roar of engines and the delicious smell of racing fuel, four riders came on to the track. Their helmets were brightly coloured, on their chests were emblazoned the Star of Norwich, or the rampant Lion of Wembley, or the Crossed Hammers of West Ham. Their leathers and machines shone like armour.

Suddenly, the starting tape flew up and the four riders raced at full speed into the first corner. Here the race was usually won or lost. The rider who got to the inside of the bend first stood the best chance of winning. The first bend was where most accidents occurred. If the inside man was going too fast and lost control of his bike he could take all the others into the fence, where they would lie spreadeagled, like knights of old, in a cloud of dust, with spinning wheels and broken bones.

Despite being such a speedway fan and admirer of the young cycle speedway racers, I was still too chicken to learn to ride my bike.

The bike remained under a potato sack amongst crates of vegetables in our tiny back yard.

THE SPIDER OF THE SPEEDWAYS

⊞▲▲▲▲▲▲▲▲▲▲▲▲▲▲▲▲▲⊞
TROUBLE FOR SHENTON.
⊞▼▼▼▼▼▼▼▼▼▼▼▼▼▼▼▼▼⊞
JIM (ROCKET) RADFORD of Bromchurch Tigers speedway club could not get Mac Shenton's warning out of his mi...
Mac ...

There was a practice for the Saturday's return match against Norburn at Norburn, and the team was chosen. Rocket Rad ford was d...

about speedway racing and about who owned the clubs."
Tom Urzetti's hands tightened which he was

The Foreman brothers.

Note the wreckage of war on the cliff face, and the gun emplacement top right.

Pud was not interested in motorbikes. He was always drawn to the sea. He and his mates built canoes from thin strips of wood and canvas. They were rather pointy and angular, not like the streamlined fibreglass canoes of today.

One day, Pud allowed me to have a go in his canoe. As a precaution he tied a long rope to the bow so I wouldn't drift too far out to sea. I paddled around for a while but when I turned towards the shore the canoe tipped over. My legs were stuck and I couldn't get out. However, I could bend my head up between my knees into the belly of the canoe where there was an air pocket, and breathe. I was aware of several people frantically splashing around me in the water for what seemed like ages.

Then suddenly the canoe was tipped the right way up and I saw Pud's shocked face. He thought he had drowned me. The last place he expected to find me was still in the canoe.

The sea was the life blood of the town and the fish market was its heart. It was the scene of unbelievable activity as herring drifters steamed and jostled for position in the crowded harbour. Baskets of fish were hauled, dripping, from the decks of the drifters, and swung across the quay and tipped into boxes. Sunlight danced across the waters of the harbour, the gleaming fish, ice and yellow waterproofs of the men. Fish scales sequined every surface. Scottish fisher-girls, who followed the shoals of herring around the coast, gutted and packed fish by the million.

Tragedy was never far from the lives of the fishermen. Several boats were lost over the years. When one sank and three members of one family were drowned (a father and two sons) we crouched under the window of the house to see if we could hear crying. It was as quiet as the grave.

We boys were at the pierhead to see the *Lord Hood* land the biggest ever single catch of herrings: 314³/₄ crans (the weight of herring is measured in crans and this quantity was equal to about 56,000 kilograms). It was feared that the weight of the catch would be too much for the vessel in the strong swell.

I was still sleeping in my mother's room, but when Pud was twenty he had to do his National Service so he married his girlfriend, Doreen, before he went. Then Ivan married his new girl, Helen, and I got their room. The brothers had slept in the big bed all their lives. Under the bed was a chamber pot, and on a little marble-topped table was a jug and basin which rattled when you walked on the cold lino floor. There was a china chicken on a china nest hatching a bar of soap.

The teacher of the top class at Pakefield Primary School was Oscar Outlaw — a big man who must have been an officer in the war. He had an air of authority which none of us would dream of challenging.

He realized that none of us had books at home. It wasn't just because of the shortage of books due to the war — we came from a culture which had no books.

Oscar Outlaw decided to rectify this by reading from his own favourite boyhood books. One day he started reading *Treasure Island*. For me the two most magical words in English Literature are 'Treasure Island'. Just to hear those words today gives me the same tingle I felt when I was first introduced to Jim Hawkins, Long John and Ben Gunn all those years ago.

I can see Oscar Outlaw now. Above his desk he was all authority, his great lion head cradled in his hands, elbows on the desk and, between his elbows, the book. But below the desk he was all little boy. His bent knees bounced up and down. His legs were in frantic motion as a duck's legs are below the surface while the body remains calm above. Oscar Outlaw was treading water so as not to drown in the excitement of the stories.

Eventually, the day we all dreaded arrived. The start of the 11+ examinations! The whole affair was a blur at the time, but I remember the spelling part. One by one we had to go to the front of the class and stand beside Oscar Outlaw as he sat at his desk. On the desk were several sheets of paper with columns of words. As he pointed to a word we had to read it. The only word I remember is the word I had never seen or heard before. 'Antiku,' I said. It was 'antique'.

There couldn't have been many households in our village where antiques were part of tea-time conversation, but if there were, those were the children the Grammar School wanted.

There were a few posh kids in the area but they went away to school, and they went away for holidays. They hardly existed for us at all. We were the 'common boys' they shouldn't play with. We could spit further, pee higher.

The posh girls went to the riding stables, run by a strapping young lady called Tessa. We called her Tessy Titswobble. When her horse trotted her bosom galloped. I thought that if her horse jumped fences, Tessa would get black eyes.

A few children passed the exam and were told they would be going to the Grammar School. A few more were in a borderline group and had to go before an interview panel who would decide if they were Grammar School material or not. I was in this group.

I dreaded this day more than the days of exams. My mother gave my plimsolls a fresh coat of whitener and gave my hair another lick. I remember being ushered into the room and a row of old faces. That's all.

At school, a few days later, I noticed Oscar having a quiet word with two or three of the children who had also been for the interview. By the end of the day he had said nothing to me. I waited for the class to empty and approached his desk. 'Please, sir. Did I pass?'

Oscar looked at me over his spectacles. 'I'm afraid not,' he said.

I ran from the room, bounded down the stairs two at a time, which wasn't allowed, and burst out through the doors into the sunshine. I leapt and jumped and whooped down the road after my friends.

I hadn't passed! I was going to the Secondary Modern School with my mates. What a relief!

Then I remembered the bike. I would have to learn to ride the bike. If I had made it to the Grammar School I could have gone by bus.

Because the bus drivers, conductors and even inspectors drank tea in our shop, they let me travel free on the buses as often as I wanted. Sometimes on rainy days I just travelled up and down the entire route for hours watching the town going about its business.

Sometimes I took Sandy, and the two of us would get off the bus at the far north end of the town where a freshwater stream ran down a wooded valley to the beach. From there we could walk further north over dunes, on to beaches I thought of as a foreign country.

Boys are very territorial. The area where they live is *their* land, and strange children wandering into it should watch out. But here, at the smart north end of town, there seemed to be no children. Perhaps the children who lived here were rich kids who were sent away to school. If there were children around, they were too polite to bother a strange boy and a dog.

I had no real ambition at this time other than the dream of going to Hollywood or playing for England, except for one day when I went to a fun-fair in Great Yarmouth. There was a striptease lady in a tent. She posed naked in a golden frame, behind a filmy sheet which made it all fuzzy and artistic. If only I was a girl, I thought; that's what I would do when I grew up.

One day, I had a new customer on my newspaper round. He came to the door as I opened the gate. He said he had just arrived in the town from Yorkshire, and asked me if there was clay in the local cliffs. I said there was and we used to dig it out and make model tanks and planes from it. We stuck matchsticks in as guns and baked them hard in our mothers' ovens.

The new customer, Tom Hudson, asked me to bring a bucket of clay to the Art School, where he was a teacher. I knew nothing about the Art School except that it was above the local Youth Club, around the corner from my barber.

When I took the clay to Mr Hudson, he decided it was too gritty for modelling, or sculpture as he called it, but suggested I join a Saturday class he was starting for school children. It was free, so I did.

He took us sketching on the first day. Unbelievably he took us to the very church orchard I had been caught scrumping in a few years before. I knew the old Dracula vicar had left the village, and had been replaced by a roly-poly vicar who liked brown ale and sing-along in the Trowel and Hammer, so I wasn't alarmed.

Sketching those gnarled old apple trees was such fun I couldn't think why I had never done it before. Drawing had always been an indoor thing, flat out on the floor in front of the fire, making things up.

Because I couldn't ride a bike I delivered the newspapers to houses nearest the shop. Other paperboys went farther afield on their bikes.

If I had been able to ride a bike, I wouldn't have had the paper round nearest the shop. I wouldn't have met Tom Hudson. I would never have gone to art school.

My family gave up trying to get me to ride my bike, and my mother sold it. I had to walk to the Secondary School, about two miles away. There was a route to the school along a narrow lane, and while all the bike riders pedalled along the roads, I walked the muddy lane and enjoyed it; swordfighting imaginary highwaymen and chopping the heads of giant cow parsley.

The school was a long, single-storeyed red brick building. At one end was the Boys' School and at the other, the Girls' School. Down the middle of the playground was an imaginary line. Girls stayed on one side and boys on the other.

Playtime was the best part of school. Children came to the school from a wide area and there were several tough boys around. The group of boys from my old school stayed together, played together and fought together. There were lots of fights in the playground.

Fights usually started as a scuffle between two boys. A ring of boys would form around them and the cry, 'A fight! A fight!' made the ring of boys swell. Sometimes other boys became involved in the fight before teachers arrived to break it up.

After such a fight involving groups of boys had been stopped by teachers, there was usually unfinished business to be settled after school. There would be threats of ambush on the way home. Being the lone walker, I was particularly concerned if our group was involved. Imaginery highwaymen and giant cow parsley I could handle, but real ambush was something else.

Possibly because we had all been friends for a long time, but probably because they delivered the newspapers for my mum, my biker friends would take the lane way home with me when an ambush was threatened.

Actually, because we had the notorious Botright brothers in our gang, we were rarely challenged.

The school was divided into four House teams, and teachers were assigned to each House. We boys didn't care which House ended the term with most House points, but to some of the teachers it seemed to be a matter of life or death. We got House points for playing in the school team, getting good marks, or for being helpful – filling the inkwells at the beginning of school, or closing the windows at the end of school.

Harry Woods, a big red-faced teacher with ginger hair and a ginger suit, was fanatical that his House should win the silver shield and only gave those jobs to boys in his House.

At about this time we got a new Headmaster. It was his first job as a Headmaster and he was full of new ideas.

He walked on to the stage on his first morning wearing his black academic gown. We were shocked. We had never seen anyone wear such a thing except in Will Hay comedy films. This man meant business. He was Michael Duane.

Brian Gifford and I painting the mural.

He wanted to brighten the place up. He asked the art teacher, Mr Nicholls, to select a couple of boys to design and paint a mural in the entrance to the school.

Mr Nicholls picked me and another boy, Brian Gifford. We did the mural of the local fishing industry: fishing boats, nets, etc. The Headmaster realized that I was good at not much beside art. He knew I was going to the Art School on Saturdays, and he arranged for me to go there two afternoons a week as well.

Most of the teachers at the Alderman Woodrow School expected little from us. The music teacher, whose name was Claude, expected more and was treated appallingly by us. He hated our accents and our manners. He was outraged if he saw us eating an apple in the street.

Claude made us push out our lips and form perfect O shapes with our mouths, then make an 'Ooh' sound, blowing gently at the same time. This, he hoped, would enable us to sing 'Nymphs and Shepherds' with a perfect BBC accent.

It all became too much for him and he left the school.

The new music teacher was very young and we treated him even worse than we had treated Claude. A few boys decided their voices were breaking so they were excused singing. Next week, we all said our voices were breaking. As we couldn't sing, the music teacher tried to tell us something of the history of music.

At some stage, and for a reason lost on me, he mentioned Michelangelo, and described him lying on his back painting the ceiling of the Sistine Chapel. From that day I was called Angelo, partly because of painting the school mural, but largely because my classmates thought I was having a lazy time at the Art School. And my name was Michael.

Some of the teachers were strict. One we respected was Arthur Rudd. We respected him because he was strict but fair. One day he discovered that none of us had read *The Wind in the Willows*. For the next few Friday afternoons he read from the book and we ruffians, big boys now with long trousers, were completely hooked by Ratty, Mole and all the inhabitants of the river bank.

When we got to the top of the school, our classroom was the one which joined the Girls' School end of the building. From our classroom we could see the girls playing netball. One girl in particular caught my attention. She was very good at netball and had a ponytail.

I found out her name was Molly. She was going out with a tall, good-looking boy in our class called Terry. He had dark, curly hair and wore a cricket sweater. He looked more like Grammar School material.

After the episode with Pud's canoe, I had no wish to have one of my own. Instead I got a lilo – an air-mattress. Although not as grown up as a canoe, it was actually more fun. Several of us could pile on at once, and you could dive from it.

One day, I was lying on my towel, stretched over the hot pebbles of the beach. In those summers the stones were sometimes too hot to walk on. People would hop and skip to the sea as if their feet were on fire. A shadow fell over me. I looked up. It was Brenda. I had sat next to Brenda for most of my years at Primary School. I had copied my sums from Brenda. Another reason I failed my exams.

She asked if she could borrow my lilo. She was wearing a shiny swimsuit with elasticated sides. When she brought the lilo back, the wet swimsuit showed the little dent of her bellybutton. Brenda had changed. I knew we would never play rugby together again.

Then I went to float on the lilo. It seemed different. It wasn't a galleon or a diving board any more. I put my head on the pillow and just lulled about on the dozing sea. Brenda had lain on my mattress . . . Then I felt a stinging pain on my face. I hadn't noticed a jellyfish tentacle clinging to the pillow.

Just when you are feeling good about a girl you get stung.

In addition to making drawings of football matches and battles, I sometimes painted posters for the shop, advertising various products, like a new washing powder or fruit drink.

One of the posh customers, Mrs Garood, thought her nephew in London should know about this. He was an executive in a big advertising agency in London and Mrs Garood arranged for Mum and me to have an interview at his office.

The school agreed for me to have a day off and we travelled up on the train. I wonder what the poor man thought of his aunt forcing him to see this little kid with his scruffy pictures.

He was very nice. We sat in his splendid office and he said I should keep drawing, study hard, and perhaps in a few years he would see me again.

I was always attracted by the graphics on the labels in the shop. Spratts dog food was my favourite.

Mum and I spent the rest of the day at the Festival of Britain. It was staged on the South Bank of the Thames (the Festival Hall is the only part of the great jamboree that remains) and was officially described as 'A Tonic for the Nation'.

Everything seemed so futuristic – except the Lion and Unicorn Pavilion, largely the work of the Royal College of Art, which was strangely Victorian.

The most spectacular structures were the Dome of Discovery, like a tied-down flying saucer, and the Skylon, balanced on wires and itching to be catapulted into space.

The stylized Britannia, designed by Abram Games as the official symbol of the 1951 Festival of Britain, appeared on everything from postage stamps to novelty souvenirs.

My lasting memories are of the special rock with the Festival symbol through the middle (Mum said it was expensive at one shilling and sixpence) and that the whole event was overcrowded and over pink. The view across the river of sooty St Paul's standing solitary among vast black bomb sites was more intriguing. I knew the bomb sites would be full of marigolds and 'common boys' inventing worlds more imaginative and lasting than the pink fly-away shapes at the Festival.

In class next day Mr Rudd asked if I had been offered the Managing Director's job at the advertising agency, ha, ha. I realized then that the teachers thought it was ridiculous that a boy like me should have such ambitions.

CAN TAKE IT

In those days very few people had cars. Only posh people. If ordinary folk wanted to go on an outing they had to go by train or coach. The old coaches were called charabancs. I don't know why, but they were fun. Occasionally on a Sunday afternoon in summer, Mum, Aunt Louie and I would go on an outing. (My brothers, Pud and Ivan, were old enough to have adventures of their own.)

We went wherever the charabanc was going. Sometimes it was a 'Mystery Tour', when only the driver knew the destination, but as the destination was always a pub, no one was worried. The outing was the thing and we would sing all the way home.

My favourite charabanc destination was a remote barn
of a pub called The Eel's Foot. It was beside a wide river,
or broad, and we could hire rowing boats and trail
arms and legs in the rippling colours of the setting sun.

Eventually Mum bought a car – a tiny Austin. Mum couldn't drive and had no intention of learning. Ivan and Pud could drive because they worked at the garage, and the plan was that they would take turns to drive Mum on outings every Sunday afternoon. The rest of us piled in the back.

Now we could go where the charabancs didn't. Best of all we could visit Granny Bacon. She was Mum's mother and was the landlady of a pub in deepest Norfolk. She was the classic country granny. Small, very tough, dressed always in black and wearing a silver brooch at her neck with the words 'Mother' on it. Her grey hair was gathered back into a bun with huge steel pins, and she wore a tall, black pointy hat.

Her mother had been landlady at the pub, and when she became too old, Granny took over. She served the customers, washed the glasses, scrubbed the brick floors and looked after the cellar, and the large family.

Grandfather had a bad leg and Granny used to smother it in a daily poultice of boiled watercress which the children had to scour the countryside to find.

Everything inside the pub seemed brown. The locals had gnarled brown hands, tobacco-stained, droopy moustaches and yellow teeth like horses. They spat plugs of chewing tobacco into the spittoons under the brown wooden settles, and their boots trailed mud over the brick floors. Even the plants on the windowsills were nicotine stained and gasped in the thick smoke, gazing longingly at the fresh air outside. When the sun came through the window it turned into a golden haze through which flitted the tiny black shadow of Granny Bacon, darting from cellar to bar with big pots of brown beer. Granny's pub, The Fox and Hounds, was one of the smells of childhood.

At the back of the pub, Granny Bacon maintained a
huge garden. Every kind of fruit, vegetable and herb
grew in wild profusion. There were golden
gooseberries as big as ping-pong balls. Bees buzzed
between bushes dangling blackcurrants and
redcurrants. Below them trailed the big leaves and
trumpet flowers of marrows and squashes. Pear trees
towered above old apple trees bent under loads of
apples with weird and wonderful names.

There was a three-holer toilet in the garden of the pub
for the customers, and a one-holer for Granny and the
family.

Big red hens hid eggs everywhere, and in the public bar, in a glass case, was an ostrich egg as big as a rugby ball. Beneath the case, old men played dominoes and I could imagine Granny Bacon giving them the odd spell along with their beer – magic potions to make their hens lay eggs as large as ostrich eggs.

177

In 1953 there was a terrible storm, and a huge tide raged down the North Sea, destroying sea defences and flooding the low land. Many people drowned along the east coast and in Holland, where the dykes burst.

The cliffs of Pakefield were high enough to prevent flooding but much of the cliff was washed away. The sea surged over the Lowestoft sea wall and through the old beach village part of the town.

No one drowned there although some of the little cottages were left full of sand and mud to a depth of several feet. Big boys were given a few days off school to help dig out the old cottages. We pretended to be an international rescue team. We were too late to save a hutch full of rabbits and lots of dolls and teddy bears.

Damaged by High Seas at Pakefield.

High Tide Damage at Pakefield, Suffolk.

As soon as I was fifteen I could leave school. With the encouragement of my Headmaster and Tom Hudson, Mum agreed that I could go full-time to the Art School. I was very lucky. I was the youngest son. Pud and Ivan were both working and earning enough to keep themselves and give some to Mum. Between them, they could afford for me to go to Art School.

On my first day I went into a drawing studio with the other students, who were two or three years older than me. A lady came in and took off all her clothes. She stood on a little box in the middle of the room.
The students stood behind easels and began to draw. I stood behind an easel in the far corner and sharpened my pencil. It kept breaking.

Because it was a very small Art School I couldn't study all the subjects I needed. So one day each week I travelled to the Art School at Great Yarmouth and sometimes to the Art School at Ipswich.

In East Anglia in the 1950s there were not many ladies around who would take off their clothes to model. In fact, Sadie was the only one. So Sadie was also in demand at the neighbouring art schools, and the two of us spent long hours cuddled up together in country buses winding along the cold, foggy roads of Norfolk and Suffolk.

Painting the same person over and over for month after month teaches you about seeing and reading colour. I had no idea there were so many pinks, blues, yellows, ochres and mauves in flesh. A couple of years later we had a new model, Lily. She was paler, cooler-coloured than Sadie and needed quite a different mix of colours. Her bone structure was more apparent. We drew all or parts of the skeleton repeatedly. The ball and socket of the thigh bone and pelvis, wrists and knuckles, elbows and ankles. It was very boring but we didn't question it.

When we came to draw and paint Lily, we saw the value of all the skeleton drawings.

November 1954

I think myself lucky to have gone to a small Art School still steeped in tradition. We studied anatomy, perspective, colour theory, the history of art and architecture. We were also out in all weathers drawing the world around us.

The Lowestoft fish market was a favourite subject. It was so noisy and frantic and friendly.

Time and again we painted the same orchard, in all seasons. The winter was best. There are so many colours in snow; so many blues, browns, reds in the black trees.

Gradually Tom Hudson led us into total abstraction. Starting with the trees in the orchard, step by step, until painting and constructing abstracts seemed natural and made perfect sense.

He urged us to draw the 'particular', the basic, the essence of a form or movement. We studied the structure of plants as we had the skeleton, opened seed pods and drew the tiny seeds very large. Isolated on paper or canvas, the seed seemed as big as the world.

At the end of my first term at the Art School a big Christmas party was organized. It was Fancy Dress and everyone had to perform a party piece. Some of the new students didn't want to do a solo performance so we decided to form a band. We had no instruments so we made our own. As I had access to biscuit tins I made drums, so I was the drummer.

When Tom Hudson added our act to the bill he wrote down 'Jazz Band'. I felt a shock of excitement. That's it. 'Jazz Band'. Of course, we were awful, but we were hooked. After the party, we all bought real instruments, except we used a tea chest and broom handle instead of double-bass. We felt this was more traditional anyway. Jazz took over from football. We were jazz fans now.

At the start of my second year, a few new students arrived. I recognized one of them. She was Molly, the girl with the ponytail.

There were two distinct groups at the local Jazz Club. One group was there for the jazz. The other group was there for the beer. There was a late licence on jazz nights so drunks could come from all the pubs around and drink later in the Jazz Club. Most of this group were young fishermen or 'fisherboys'.

The 'teddy boys' in the mid 1950s adopted a unique clothes style. They wore long drape jackets with lapels and cuffs in contrasting colours, narrow 'drain pipe' trousers and big suede shoes with thick crêpe soles. On the front of the shoe there was often a glittery chain. Their shirts were plain coloured, pink or pale yellow with a narrow 'slim jim' tie or a 'bootlace' tie.

In our area, the fisherboys had their own distinctive fashion too. Their jackets were similar in shape to the teds', but even more special, with double pleats in the back and a half belt. The trousers were the opposite of drain pipes, and had very wide legs. They were very expensive. The fisherboys, like generations of seamen before them, wore a single earring (forty years before earrings became trendy). Earrings were worn by seafarers to pay for a proper Christian burial should their bodies be washed up on a foreign shore.

The fisherboys were often at sea for many days and nights in harsh and dangerous conditions. When they came ashore for a day or two, they had a pocket full of money and a short time in which to spend it. They lavished their hard-earned cash on suits, girlfriends and a good time.

Many of my schoolmates became fisherboys. I envied them their money, but not their life on the rough, freezing North Sea.

There were frequent fights between the 'fisherboys' and the 'teddy boys', but the musicians were usually regarded as neutrals. But one night while our band was playing the fight erupted onto the stage.

Mike, our clarinet player, always stared into space while he played. During one long solo he was staring vacantly as usual when one of the fisherboys took exception. He thought Mike was staring at his glass eye. The fisherboy leapt on to the stage and butted Mike in the face. He was followed by several of his brothers, all notoriously violent, and the rest of the fisherboys.

Drums and bodies rolled around the floor as the teddy boys waded in, and the musicians, all notoriously timid, escaped. Except Colin, our vegetarian pacifist banjo player who stayed behind to point out that fighting was silly.

Our band never got better than awful, but we got 'gigs' as the interval band at various pubs and clubs. Of course, the interval was when everyone went to the bar to get more drink, so very few people ever heard how bad we were.

The best 'gigs' were the 'Riverboat Shuffles', named after the traditional riverboats which carried bands and revellers up and down the Mississippi. Our boats were the last of the lovely old steamers which chugged along the River Waveney and into the network of broads. There would be two or three bands on board, crates of beer and mad dancing. The boat stopped at remote waterside pubs where we played and drank and sailed home in the dark.

The Jazz Club became a weekly haunt for us. Most of the art students went there, including Molly. I tried to think of ways to impress her. Maybe, I thought, next time we go sketching on the pier she might fall in and I could rescue her and have an excuse to talk to her.

But one night, Molly and I didn't go to the pub. Everyone else had gone but I found myself standing on a corner with Molly and her drop handlebar racing bike. We seemed to talk for ages. It was misty and cold. I don't know what we talked about. Then she kissed me, hopped on her bike and disappeared into the mist.

I ran down the road, leaping in the air and punching the overhanging autumn leaves. I ran all the way home without touching the ground. The last time I had been kissed was by my brother Ivan's friend Bob's wife at her wedding when I was nine years old.

Then gloom, fear. If I was to 'go out' with Molly, I would have to learn to ride a bike . . .